Otherwise
Engaged

Otherwise
Engaged

Suzanne Finnamore

Alfred A. Knopf *New York 1999*

THIS IS A BORZOI BOOK
PUBLISHED BY ALFRED A. KNOPF, INC.

MAY 1 2 1999

Copyright © 1999 by Suzanne Finnamore

All rights reserved under International and Pan-American
Copyright Conventions. Published in the United States by
Alfred A. Knopf, Inc., New York, and simultaneously in
Canada by Random House of Canada Limited, Toronto.
Distributed by Random House, Inc., New York.

www.randomhouse.com

Owing to limitations of space, all permissions to reprint
previously published material will be found on page 213.

Knopf, Borzoi Books, and the colophon are registered
trademarks of Random House, Inc.

Library of Congress Cataloging-in-Publication Data
Finnamore, Suzanne.
Otherwise engaged / Suzanne Finnamore. — 1st ed.
p.   cm.
ISBN 0-375-40652-2 (alk. paper)
I. Title.
PS3556.I4965O44   1999
813'.54—dc21   98-49998
CIP

Manufactured in the United States of America

First Edition

for Mark

Otherwise
Engaged

October

The female of the species is more deadly than the male.

RUDYARD KIPLING

He did it. I said yes and checked my watch. 7:22 p.m.

I sneak a pen out of my purse and write the time down on the palm of my hand, in what I hope is a nonchalant fashion. I am excited and at the same time I feel there is a possibility of an inquiry.

He didn't kneel. It's unlikely I would marry someone who did. From then on, I would live in fear of Whitman's Samplers. Tandem bicycles. Someone who knelt would need me to give up my name and bake pies while his aging mother cried out in pain from the next room.

Exhilaration. Also something darker: a sense of triumph. It is primal, furtive; my ovaries cracking cheap champagne. I win. Those two words; that's exactly how I feel. Happy, but not in an I Knew It All Along way. Definitely in a Contestant Who Has Won in the Final Round Despite Major Setbacks way.

And the Harvard professors who say a woman is as likely to be married after thirty-five as to be abducted by terrorists? May they fall into open manholes, where hard-body lesbians with blowtorches await them.

I am thirty-six years of age.

I need to write it all down. Exactly what was said, exactly what happened.

It all began Sunday morning. I woke up and heard him padding around the kitchen of our San Francisco flat: making coffee, unfolding his *New York Times*. Sun dappled the crisp two-hundred-thread-count cotton sheets. Outside the bedroom window, two finches nuzzled on a branch. In the kitchen, Molly O'Neill was freeing kumquats from their humdrum lives. At that moment I decided it probably wasn't going to get any better than this. The free introductory trial period was over.

He brought in my coffee, murmuring the theme song from *Goldfinger*.

"Goldfinger . . . he's the man, the man with the Midas touch . . . the spider's *touch*."

He was planning his day. It was going to be a day like any other. It would be free of confrontation, conflict, or commitment, anything that could remotely lead to a subpoena. Michael is what his therapist calls change averse. The survivor of a bitter divorce, which he refers to simply as The Unpleasantness.

The day he had planned was going to include me, but it was going to revolve around him. Just a nice Sunday is what he would have called it.

It was my task to set the earth spinning the other way.

I took his hand, and said, "You know what?" Pleasantly, as though I had some interesting good news to share with him.

"You need to decide about us. Now."

He tensed, his eyes flitting around the room. A paperboy caught in the grip of a mad clown.

There ensued a period of silence. He stared past my right shoulder, transfixed by a point just outside the present. He had decided to go blank.

I cataloged events for him, since he was so bad with time.

"We've known each other three years. We've been living together six months."

I asserted that I wasn't going to be like Gabrielle, the hair model who lived with him for four years and got the Samsonite luggage.

"I love you," I said. "But I can't just stay in limbo."

What's wrong with limbo? I heard him thinking. Limbo is fantastic.

"Especially if we want to have children," I said.

His face went white. He had understood that one word, "children." Ten years ago his first wife, Grace, left him and moved to Vermont along with Michael's three-year-old daughter, Phoebe. Every year, Michael cries on her birthday. Phoebe calls her stepfather Daddy, and Michael, Michael.

"I understand if you can't move forward," I said. Beat. Sip of coffee. Sad smile. "But I have to."

I added that if he didn't marry me, he would probably end up alone. A few meaningless and shallow affairs with a certain type.

"Users," I said. "Women who don't want a commitment."

His face, I thought, lit up.

"An old man in a rocking chair," I said. "Eating Dinty Moore beef stew out of cans."

This is what he eats when I am gone. This and corn. Michael turned forty-four last July. Together we are about a hundred.

"We're meant to be together," I said. "But if not you, I'll move on and find someone else."

I wondered how many women were lying that same lie at that exact moment. In truth he would have to blast me out with dynamite, just like Gabrielle. Holding on to the front doorjamb with the tips of my fingers and screaming. Hooking my feet around the wrought-iron banister.

He said he would think it over. The fact that he had to think it over made me want to cry and break things. I looked out the window. The birds were gone.

"I guess I always knew it would come to this," he pronounced, deadpan.

He slumped quietly out the door and I heard his motorcycle start up. I looked out the window as he drove away. He had his full-face Shoei helmet on. He looked like a large blue-headed beetle, moving away at high speed. The way he was going, one might think he would never return. But just like the little rubber ball attached to the toy paddle with a long elastic string and a single staple, he has to come back. All his things are here.

When he returned four hours later we both pretended it hadn't happened. I roasted a chicken; we ate it in front of *60 Minutes*. I commented on how fine Ed Bradley looked. How tall and sleek, like a panther. Michael is five foot nine, Caucasian. Serial dreams of being in the NBA.

The following day he left for an overnight business trip to Colorado. The timing was impeccable. One night to think things over, to imagine a world without a sun. That night he called me from his hotel in Denver, saying there was something he wanted to talk about when he got back. Code word: "Something."

"Have a safe trip home," I said. "Darling."

I hung up and made reservations at the Lark Creek Inn in Marin. Chef Bradley Ogden, home of the eighteen-dollar appetizer. That night I sleep fitfully. I am what my mother used to call overexcited. I think about what if the plane crashes and he never gets to ask me. I will tell people he did, I decide.

I felt extremely focused.

The next day, Tuesday. He comes home around four in the afternoon. He actually runs to the kitchen, to find me.

He loves me, I am thinking. Also: Baby, you are going *DOWN*.

We embrace. His skin feels cool, as though he had flown home without the airplane. He has on a thick moss-green plaid flannel shirt which he has purchased in Santa Fe, probably in a Western store with a wooden Indian outside. It soothed him, buying that shirt. I can see that.

At six we dress for dinner in silence. I watch him. And when I see him pull his gray suit out of the armoire, I know. It's not his best suit, but it's my favorite. Single-breasted. With the suit, he puts on his black merino-wool sweater. Another clue. A simple shirt would've been one thing. Or a black knit tee. The black tee would say, I'm sporty but not serious. It would say, I know how to wear a tee shirt with a suit, I'm a good catch. Try and catch me. The merino sweater has a collar and three neat buttons. It says, I'm caught. And I'm taking it like a man.

I wear a black sheer-paneled skirt and a long knit jacket from my first trip to Paris. Black hose, black heels. I put on my earrings with my eyes still on him. I hook the wire through the hole, blind.

We drive across the Golden Gate Bridge without speaking. Black Saab, top down. I'm wearing a velvet hat and dark sunglasses. We are listening to the jazz station. This would make a good commercial, is what I'm thinking. Also I am wondering how I am going to live if he doesn't ask. We would have to break up immediately, tonight. This instant. My mind flips back and forth, a fish on the deck.

We arrive and valets grab the keys from his hand, open doors. Once inside, we are quickly seated. Time is speeding up, not slowing down as in emergencies. Table in the corner. The perfect table, I am thinking. Now he has to ask me. The center tables are ambiguous. The corner tables are definite.

They pour the wine. He tastes it, nodding. He orders our food; I let him. I can't feel my legs.

There is a long, flesh-eating silence.

And then he says, "So what should we do?"

"About what?" I ask, caressing the stem of my glass. I am going to make this as difficult as possible for him, I don't know why. There seem to be bonus points involved.

"You know what," he says.

He has a wide, strange smile, like a maniac who is about to reveal that he is strapped full of Plastique explosives.

"What what?" I ask.

Now I am smiling too. I can't help it.

"Maybe we should get engaged." He says it.

"Maybe we should," I say.

I take a long slow sip of wine. I have seen our cat, Cow Kitty, whom we call the Cow for short, do this to bees. First he stuns them and then he watches them die.

"Do I have to do it now?" Michael asks. He sees the waiter headed toward us, a large tray held expertly overhead. He has ordered the Yankee Flatiron Pot Roast, with baby vegetables. $28.95. "Can't we wait until after?" he says.

"No. You have to ask me now," I say. The pot roast is an incentive, making sure it's hot when he eats it. I'll get this out of the way, he's thinking, and then there will be pot roast.

"Will you marry me?" he says.

"Yes," I say.

We kiss. People around us continue to eat. It seems there should be something else, but there isn't. It's just a question, after all. Five words, including the answer. The pot roast arrives and he eats it all. I barely touch my cod; it is impossibly pale. I can see the plate through it. It occurs to me that I may be dreaming. I pinch my arm.

"What are you smiling at?" he asks.

"Nothing," I say. I'm awake, I don't say.

I always thought I would cry. But I don't. I laugh.

Later we get on the speaker phone and call my mother, who lives in Carmel with my stepfather, Don. She whoops.

It's difficult not to feel insulted. We finally found a buyer for the Edsel.

All night, I envision my future life. I lie faceup on the bed, like an egg. I baste in entitlement.

Considerable lifetime benefits apply as Michael's wife. His French onion soup, the Julia Child recipe with home-made beef stock. An exhaustive two-day ritual from which he consistently emerges embittered, swearing this is really the last time. The very last.

Now he will have to make it, despite threats to the con-trary. As his wife I could leave him, and take things that are his with me.

I mentally pore over my haul, fanning the Halloween candy out to gloat.

His eyes are the color of caramel, with a ring of hazel. His skin smells clean, like paper. The thick brown kind, from grade school. His skin smells like a good memory. If I can keep part of me in contact with it, I have the impression I will never be harmed.

Listening to him impersonate people we know, while we are lying in bed. Male or female, he is equally proficient. In addition he does the voice of the Cow so you think that must be what his voice really is.

I write ads for athletic shoes; Michael is a marketing director across town. Since he makes more money than I do, I could quit my job, for about three weeks. At that point the people from American Express would begin to arrive in heli-copters. Still. I could never do that before.

Once when I was away on a long television campaign shoot in Morocco, he drank martinis and overate red meat at Izzy's every night until the very last day, and then he got a migraine and went to emergency. They gave him Dem-erol and sent him home. When I arrived home he gave me his hospital wristband, and called it Jewish jewelry.

He takes me out to dinner in the middle of the week, saying, "I'm taking you out to dinner." When I'm depressed, he makes me a soft-boiled egg in a cup, with buttered toast fingers.

There are also the long-term aspects. The Not Dying a Bitter Old Maid with a Companion Dog thing.

Actually I've thought about it and if I die I want to be incinerated and then immediately scattered. I don't want anyone looking at my dead body, especially Michael. I don't like the idea of not being able to suck in my stomach or slant my hips.

What is this "if"? I am going to die. But I will die married, unless it doesn't work out. In that case, I would have to scramble for a replacement Michael. This would not be easy.

He does a chilling Deepak Chopra.

This is not my first engagement.

I have a photograph of myself at twenty-seven, thinner and with long hair, holding up a butterfish on a pier in Lake Tahoe, Nevada. I am standing alongside my semiprofessional basketball player ex-boyfriend, the one who used to strangle me.

He was the first man to ever propose. It was 1986, and we were tweaking on cocaine at his house in the Berkeley hills. We had just swallowed a Quaalude apiece, to take the edge off the coke. I swallowed the Quaalude, he asked me, and I said yes.

He looks happy in the photograph and so do I. I once saw him vomit into the kitchen trash can, and a moment later continue to mix drinks.

When he gave me a black eye, I left him.
But thanks for asking, in other words.

I went to look at rings, at Tiffany's. Alone. I wanted to get the lay of the land.

A Chinese man with a terrible wig sells me up to a twenty-thousand-dollar ring. A wide platinum band with a huge white diamond slid into it. I have a hard time taking it off. I keep looking at myself in the mirror, with my hand held on my cheek like an Oil of Olay ad.

The ring twinkles madly. It seems to whisper, *Hey girl. You really deserve me.*

Everything else is really going to be a letdown, after me.

I am the IT ring.

Nearby a woman with a thick Southern accent is laughing softly and explaining how she can't consider anything less than three carats. The saleswoman, a tall woman with Teutonic high cheekbones and black-rimmed glasses, nods in tacit agreement. Her blond chignon is wound tight as her smile. Yes, I imagine her saying, the children too. Everyone into the ovens.

As I leave Tiffany's, I walk past the security man with the tinted glasses. He looks at me. I immediately look down. I notice that the carpets are stained.

I am pretty sure that Audrey Hepburn would not be caught dead here.

Everyone asks the same two questions.

"Did you know he was going to do it?"

"I had a feeling," I say. My eyes slide sideways of their own accord.

They launch the second question right away.

"Have you set a date?"

"October nineteenth, of next year."

I feel spared. My perception is that if you don't have a date, they stone you.

We went to look at rings together, at Shreve's. Since 1852. Michael said if we found something, we could buy it today. I felt I had just won a game show. It was all I could do to keep from skipping down the aisle.

Earlier this morning, I confessed to Michael I had fallen in love with the Chinese wig man Tiffany ring. I mentioned the twenty-thousand-dollar price. He assured me that this would never happen.

Then when we got to Shreve's, he was more than happy to fork over seven thousand dollars for the one I really wanted. The ring is my lump-sum payment for everything bad that has ever happened to me. I don't feel I can tell people this, or they will spoil it.

I found it last week, when I cased the place alone. It meets all the minimum requirements for Cut, Color, and Clarity, as outlined by our salesman, Reed Cashman, who looks like an international spy posing as a diamond sales-man. It's a carat, in a simple four-prong solitaire setting.

That's a lie. It's .81 carat. I round up.

My mother called this morning to brief me on a fight she has had with Don. It was about his underwear being dyed pink.

"Accidentally," she adds.

She has done this before. Never her underwear, always his. It's not a mistake; it's repertoire.

"What would Freud say?" I ask.

"What did Freud know about laundry?" she asks. "Screw Freud."

This seems to settle things.

We exchange stories of malcontent fashioned from the oddments of our lives as women. She tells me about the laundry fight. I tell her about the commitment wars.

We are coming home from dinner. Michael has broken up with Gabrielle, in the Longest Breakup in the History of the World. She has moved out of his flat, and after a suitable period of insensate philandering, Michael has been dating me for six months. A quantity of wine has gone by from a place called Frog's Leap.

The word "commitment" is brandished.

"You're afraid of commitment," I pronounce.

Silence.

"You'll never change," I say. "You don't want to build anything."

Michael says nothing, but continues to drive very carefully. There is a bomb in the car, his movements suggest.

"Fine," I pronounce. "You should just be alone, then."

Being with me is his only option. Distantly I know this is flawed logic, but I don't have time to work it out. I slam out of the car and hurry up the front steps of my building. My high heels make a good sound on the marble. At this point I am completely in the moment, just doing the scene. It's as Andy Warhol said: When I open my eyes, the movie begins.

I reach the door. Hand on the knob, I mentally preview the remainder of the night: alone, chain-smoking, waiting all night for the apology call. Which doesn't come, because he hasn't actually done anything. Which is the problem. He never does anything, which lends itself to me doing all sorts of things.

I dash back down the stairs.

As I hit the street, his turn signal is blinking. Small terrifying puffs of smoke are coming from his exhaust pipe. His car inches forward, about to pull out into traffic. I begin to run, realizing how foolish I look. A large truck with the words ENJOY LIFE, EAT OUT MORE OFTEN roars by, delaying him by the necessary seconds. I reach the car and grasp the handle of his door, as if to stop it by physical force. I remember thinking that if I had to, I would.

We look at each other through the glass. He stops the car, but does not roll his window down.

"Hey," I say; it is all I can think of. Plus I'm out of breath. And drunk. I'm fairly certain of that now.

His face doesn't change expression as his arm reaches around to unbuckle his seatbelt. I keep my eyes trained on his arm. If I look away he will change his mind.

That night he tells me he loves me, for the first time.

"Why?" I ask.

"Because you ran."

I met Michael at a Christmas party in 1992. We were introduced by Lesli, an agency producer I worked with at the time. He was alone, although Lesli informed me that he was living with a Frenchwoman whom he might marry. Then where is she? I thought, ever the mercenary. I felt it was like someone leaving an Italian greyhound tied loosely to a parking meter outside a liquor store: foolish.

I had seen him before, black haired, handsome, wearing a worn leather jacket and heavy dark boots, carrying a motor-cycle helmet. Slouching up against a pillar inside the ad agency where I worked, knowing of course how the helmet helped, along with his unfamiliarity, his Guest Star sheen. He was freelancing there, getting twelve hundred a day to consider new and exciting ways to market salad oil, to make salad oil huge. I found it charming, his willingness to discuss things nobody else wanted to discuss. His eagerness to survive.

Michael has that. You get the feeling that if you were with him and you were taken hostage by terrorists with red bandannas, you would be among the few to escape. And that while you were waiting to escape, you would somehow be made comfortable.

And now here he was, at this Christmas party. Unattended.

Over icy Cosmopolitans in martini glasses, I discovered that he was Jewish, age forty-one, born in 1951: an age I found personally challenging and mysterious. After thirty-three years of being single, I had exhausted the '64s, the '62s, the '58s and the '57s. It was inevitable that I would get around to tasting the '51s. *Musty, but with an oaky finish that unfolds nicely on the tongue. Good complexity. Stands up well into '99. Drink now.*

As an extra incentive, Michael was also convinced by Lesli to give me a ride home, except he didn't, exactly. He meandered around San Francisco, hopelessly lost. I thought at the time he was flirting, but now I know he was really lost; Michael couldn't find his way out of a tunnel. As he careened from one irrevocable one-way street to another, we burrowed deep in conversation, braying at each other's jokes with the enthusiasm of men and women who don't know one another. I didn't care what direction we were going, or if in fact the car was moving at all. We were having fun, and at thirty-three and forty-one, respectively, that was dangerous. At that stage in my life, I would kill for fun. I would lock a stranger in a car trunk and drive away laughing madly into the night, deciding against punching airholes.

He drove me back to my car, but then at the last moment he suggested we go for a drink, which seemed to only reinforce the idea that our real lives didn't have to resume. Not while there was still a bar left open in San Francisco.

We sat across the marbled bar at Il Fornaio looking intently at one another, burning holes in each other's eyes. We drank fine white wine in thin Italian goblets. We warmed to our topics. We spoke of William Burroughs and Robert Mapplethorpe and Barbara Kruger. We evoked the gods of apathy: Warhol. Capote. Updike. Kerouac. We bandied slivers of monologue by David Mamet and Spalding Gray. There was very little that could stop us as we went on to our stories of personal travel, engulfed in a cloud of blissful pretense. There should be a police force to govern the upwardly mobile and stop them when they get like this, when we start to believe that we are well read and well traveled and that knowledge is within reach. They should come up to you just as you're sipping your Pinot Grigio and quoting Nabokov and they should hit you in the face with a bat. It really would be better for everyone concerned.

But nobody stopped Michael and me. Then, abruptly, he opened his wallet, drawing out a small photograph. It was a picture of his daughter leaning on a snowboard. Phoebe.

We talked on. He said that after two years with a French hair model named Gabrielle, he was in a period of domestic confusion. He made it sound as if he had a wonderful yet clumsy maid whom he might have to let go. He was, the tilt of his eyebrows suggested, waiting to see if she improved. He hoped that she would.

I remember how I drank him all in, that night, like a tulip glass of fine port. He looked both tired and supremely relaxed. His whole face seemed to recline in an expression of relaxation and hidden reserves of carnal expertise. Anyone able to write strategies for the Wesson Family of Oils is arguably prodigious, perhaps even sensual. His whole being seemed comfortably forty-one, and slightly tanned. He was a tawny port.

I looked at Michael and I saw the epitome of Nice Jewish Man spread out before me. I took in the trim watch, the good shoes carefully brushed, the lines of patience around the eyes. From her kitchen in Carmel, my mother held up a wooden spoon in silent praise of the man that sat before me discussing opera. A wave of psychic enthusiasm passed over our heads from Carmel. My mother has wanted a nice Jewish man for me since before the beginning of time. She has wanted that since before the earth was a cloud of gas.

I knew then, arranging myself at the bar stool so my DKNY Nude legs were at their best advantage, that sophistication and adoration and my mother's eternal blessing could be mine. If only I could eliminate Gabrielle. I took a sip of wine and backed a steamroller over her in my mind. I mentally placed us all on a vacation in Paris, where Gabrielle was from, a foreign country where they understood crimes of passion. I would ensconce myself in a hotel room adjacent to theirs. When she went out for baguette, I would pounce, some blunt object in hand. Perhaps a large hair dryer.

I saw her pinwheeling down the steps at Montmartre, flailing lifeless past the French carousel as the painted horses laughed silently and ironically. Afterward, Michael and I would accidentally meet as he walked along the Seine, and discuss his grief. Her family, of course, would handle the arrangements. We would check into the Hôtel Montalembert, because he would need to change hotels after what had happened, and it would be better if he weren't alone.

It wouldn't even have to be Paris, I thought. It could happen anywhere, anytime.

I wanted very badly, as Michael leaned forward across the bar and told me tales of contemporary literature, to look up and see her coffin being transported down Battery Street while a bevy of musicians played a gay Creole funeral march. I was deep in a fantasy without the hindrance of moralistic ceilings. Cardiac arrest, brain aneurysms, clinical diabetes. All of these danced like sugarplums out of my reach. I had no way to rid myself of Gabrielle. She had possession.

By midnight, we had discussed all topics that reflected well on either of us. We had held up the mirror of mutual narcissism and had not been found wanting. But it was aborted by the fact that he, Michael, had the lack of foresight to choose Gabrielle a full two years before we had been brought together by Fate. I tried not to loathe him for his insistence on having a life before meeting me, but it was difficult.

I told him that I wanted to say something. When I drink too much wine I start to announce my sentences before they appear. He slouched forward in the solicitous way that charming men have, the way that suggests that they were just marking time until they spoke with you, marking time their whole lives.

I said, "I think you're intelligent and funny and handsome. And I wish you were single." I thought I was being boldly confiding. In retrospect, I realize it was like saying, *You know, there is air all around us.*

He jammed his hands into his pockets, as if searching for a tidbit there that would satisfy. A minute talisman of truth which he could present in lieu of a response. Maybe he had small slips of paper with quotes from eighteenth-century poets in his pockets, waiting to be pulled forth as pithy offerings. But no. He had only credit cards and a California driver's license with his photograph and the word "Taken."

He decided, in the end, to save himself. He armed himself with the shield of ambiguity. Michael ran his tongue over his teeth thoughtfully. He then replied, "You may not hear from me for a long time."

A good job, under the circumstances. Michael had managed to infer that he would be coming for me at some later time, and yet he had said nothing of the kind. He had kept himself clean. Not many men could do as much given the length of the evening, the wine consumed, and the reaction time allotted.

I admired Michael then, for all of his skills, even the ones he showed in maneuvering around me. Talking to him was deeply satisfying. Being with him held a natural pleasure. Perhaps he is gay, I thought.

But driving home alone that night, I knew two things for certain. Number one, Michael wasn't gay. And, number two, I had met the man I was going to marry.

The next morning I drove to see my mother in Carmel. I sat in her kitchen, hungover and exhausted, and wept into my hands.

"What if he doesn't leave her," I said.

"He will," she said.

Three and a half years later, he proposed.

My mother is a witch. Not a make-believe witch, not someone who dresses in black and attends outdoor all-woman festivals on the solstice. An actual witch.

Someone who knows.

Picked up the ring today. We have drinks at Le Central to celebrate. Michael has a Manhattan, which they bring in a small clear carafe with its own little ice bucket.

We make a toast.

"To us," he says. We kiss.

Admiring the ring, I hold my arm outstretched, as if stopping traffic from advancing forward.

At the table next to us sits an older businessman with his mistress. She has thick platinum hair and a fur stole. He keeps patting her hand and calling her Sweetheart. I see the intelligence of a fox in her eyes. She smokes and watches me with great amusement.

This is all a show, her eyes suggest. We might just as well be one another.

Today I bought my first issue of *Modern Bride* magazine, the November issue. I have it right here. I ordered a year's subscription using the 1-800 number and not the business reply mail card.

Your Dream Dress (It's Here!)
50 Romantic Honeymoons—from Sweet to Sexy
12 Reception Hints You Can't Overlook
6 Real Bridal Makeovers with Expert Tips for You

I discover that holding the magazine makes me anxious. I put it down. I am wondering if there is a way to make me over and, if so, will I be able to be made back.

It strikes me that I am going to have to have a wedding. And it is going to have to be perfect, according to this magazine. There are twelve reception hints I can't overlook. And that's just the tip of the bayonet.

My gut feeling is, My *God*, haven't I done enough?

November

To look back is to relax one's vigil.

BETTE DAVIS

Morning. Behind the door of our only bathroom, I hear Michael brushing his teeth with his ultrasound toothbrush. It sounds as though he is filing them to points. In our rifle-shaped Victorian flat, six small rooms all choked together, I can hear everything he does. And he can hear me. We perform behind scrims.

The water is turned on in the sink, a slow stingy stream. He begins to shave. I would like to watch, but he has locked me out, along with the Cow. This is a sacred place, a site of ritual. We are none of us worthy.

Next comes the lengthy hot bath, with the loofah. He rubs his entire body with a loofah mitt. Later I hear the shower running. After draining the tub, he stands under the shower and washes his hair twice. Lather, rinse, repeat. I never repeat.

He suffers, he is the first to point out, from acute dry skin. In winter, once a month he puts a special gel on his scalp and wears a shower cap to bed. Then I call him Do-Rag Man, and if he's in a good mood he'll sing to me in bed, in the voice of Paul Robeson.

I can always find a man with perfect skin. But where else will I find a man who can sing Negro spirituals?

Rain tonight, our first of the season. I came home and made Cornish game hens with potatoes and rosemary. We ate in the kitchen.

I put on a cassette tape of Tony Bennett, "I Left My Heart in San Francisco," which was my father's favorite song. I start to cry. Michael looks alarmed, drops his fork, and runs over to my side of the table.

"Sweetie, what's wrong?"

"I'm just so happy," I say. I feel this is a delayed reaction, like in trauma victims. I've been hit.

He brings me a paper towel and sits back down. Then he smiles apologetically and tucks into his potatoes.

We have lit candles, tonight. I hope we will always remember to do this, but even as I hope this I know that we won't. We will forget.

My ring throws off prisms of light. When I drive in the morning especially, I love watching the tiny rainbows splay across the leather interior of my car. I may die that way, staring at the ring. Plowing head-on into a semi, entranced. Exactly what such a person deserves.

Out in the world, everyone concentrates on the minu-
tiae of the wedding. The dress, the caterers. People are
concerned about place cards. It's like they don't watch the
news.

"Are you going to wear white?" a woman I hardly know
asks me. It is clear from the menacing tilt of her head that
she expects an answer.

Without thinking, I say no. Cream, is what I say. Inside I
am astounded that this matters, that it would even come up.
I am even more surprised that I have an opinion. Cream.

Yesterday I met my friend Beth for lunch at Grumpy's.
Beth is a recovering shopaholic who looks like Michelle
Pfeiffer, except with very short white-blond hair and a scar
on one cheek from when she went through the windshield at
age five. Beth was eighty thousand dollars in debt at twenty-
five; she's been credit card free for ten years. I met her at
Macy's in 1989, where we were both buying vacuums. She
said she was only allowed to do that because she was paying
cash and because hers had blown up when she tried to suck
up a whole bag of cat litter. I remember thinking, Finally.
Someone I can relate to.

Over lunch, Beth tells me that she and her husband,
Robert, don't have sex anymore. She says it was never that
great, and since Max was born, they don't do it at all.

"But hey," she says. "Sex isn't everything."

This disturbs me. Because I know, actually, that it is. Yet
when she says this, I nod. It is important to me that Beth and
Robert do not break up. They are one of the couples I need
to believe are happy in order to pioneer my own happiness. I
don't want them to get divorced. I don't want anyone to get
divorced.

Then she says she truly loves Robert. She says it with her eyebrows raised, daring me to object.

I smile, robotic. I am thinking that she is only thirty-five. I am thinking that while sex isn't everything, it's not nothing either: there should be a minimum.

Beth has the mushroom gardenburger. She puts extra salt on her fries and eats them one by one, pressing them against the bottom of her plate to pick up the extra grains.

"I do miss sex." She sighs, as though it were a dog that ran away.

After lunch I go back to my office, close the door, and eat four chocolate SnackWell sandwich cookies.

Michael and I will be different. I will wish it so. Like in a dream where you realize you're dreaming, and you can change things.

Michael works on a variety of packaged-goods accounts, the biggest of which is Sara Lee, home of the Rich Buttery Taste. Watching phyllo dough triangles tumble off a cookie sheet all day long can be less interesting than you'd think, yet he goes in every day, at 8 a.m. I sleep for another hour and then I get up and go to my own job, in advertising. What my partner Graham calls *another room in hell*.

Graham is a twenty-five-year-old art director, the other half of our creative team. He was raised in London. His parents are around four hundred years old apiece and used to sit at home reading the *Times* with him when he was two. Then Graham grew up and moved to San Francisco and became an art director, and my first boss Katherine hired him. Then she hired me and put us together on the California Lottery account. It was all arranged before we were born.

Graham is small and wan with ice-blue eyes. His hair is orange and he wears baggy pants that almost fall off. At first glance Graham looks like a paperboy, but when you look into his eyes he turns into the head of the CIA. He can draw a razor-straight line freehand and knows how to say no to people who come from upstairs.

I rationalize that I am making advertising less awful, that the work Graham and I do is less harmful and more enlightened, because we do pro bono public service announcements for AIDS awareness and fund-raising ads for public zoos, which when you think about it are the most nihilistic fascists going and might as well exhibit their leopards in boxcars. But all that's really a rationalization. I'm right in there, grinding it out. I'm every bit as disgusting as the people who do the cartoon cigarette billboards aimed toward minors and the makers of matchbooks that promise artistic fame and say, Can You Draw Binky?

Today Graham is at an edit session for a television commercial we have created for high-top basketball shoes. In a time-honored ritual, the art director is forced to stand by and watch as his meticulously designed scenes are questioned, maimed, and ultimately destroyed by a brand manager who swoops into the editing bay at the last minute. At this time, the company logo is customarily adjusted to fill the screen.

Graham called me toward the middle of the ritual, and whimpered in the dulcet tones of the Beaten Down. He was, however, cheered by the fact that I have spent my morning making long-distance personal phone calls and watching Kurosawa's *Ran* on the VCR monitor in our office with the sound turned off, to the tune of *The Best of Tom Jones* played at top volume on the CD player. He feels that by doing this instead of writing shoebox copy, I am letting freedom ring.

Graham has an expression for anything that keeps one away from the creation of advertising. He calls it a Harm Umbrella. We try to get under it as often as possible. We have similar goals, which are to do as little as possible, to get paid as much as possible, and to complain constantly while this is going on.

It's not all leisure. Often we work furiously against a strategy that doesn't exist, for clients we don't have. Yesterday we spent the morning concepting new slogans for the International Prune Board.

Prunes. Join The Movement!

Go Ahead, Make A Splash . . . With Prunes.

Little. Black. Wrinkled. Prunes!

Prunes . . . They Used To Be Plums.

So Delicious, You Could Eat Them Like Candy. But Don't.

Our favorite game is Outlate. This is where we, on regular workdays when we're not away on production, attempt to outlate each other. Like I'll come in at 9:45, and maybe Graham has just come in five minutes earlier, at 9:40. The next day I come in at 10; he comes in at 10:20. The next day I figure maybe about 10:55, so I time it perfectly, and just as I see him coming around the corner in his lime-green convertible, I drive around the block a few times, go to the bank and get a latte at the coffee stand next to the ATM; but when I get to work, he's still not there. He's gone out for a full breakfast. So the next day I come in at 11:30, quarter to 12. Graham tools in after lunch, carrying a shopping bag from Pottery Barn.

That is why he's the champion.

. . .

Chicken has become an issue. I want it twice a week; Michael gets tired after once. I feel starved for chicken; he feels chicken is keeping him from the cornucopia of life.

I talked to Reuben about it, at our therapy session yesterday. Reuben is a seventy-year-old Marin County prominent Jungian. That's how I describe him to people: a seventy-year-old Marin County prominent Jungian. I've been seeing him since last month, when I started to feel like I was flying apart. I tell myself it's just the engagement, but of course it isn't. It's the fact that I am not remotely, as Anne Lamott would say, *well* enough to be doing this.

Reuben said that when people get engaged, conflict comes bubbling to the surface. He said that while seemingly petty, it hides something deeper. That it's our job as a couple to find out what that is. That it's probably a very old story, from our childhood, and has nothing to do with the other person.

Then he splayed his fingers together into an arch, and said, "Plato believed that all human beings live in a cave, and all they can see are the shadows that they themselves cast against the wall.

"We never get to see the full picture," he explained.

"Then what am I doing here?" I ask.

We both pretend that I am joking.

It's 1 a.m. and I'm awake, stealing time. Michael's sleeping, making the faraway train sound with his breath. I enjoy hearing men sleep. It's a shame they can't do more of it, or even occasionally lapse into a mini-coma, and the women would get to be free for a few days. We could wake them up by ringing a bell of some sort.

I stare at the apricot walls. Months it's been, here in the two-bedroom one-bath Victorian flat with the crazy South African landlady upstairs, who gardens in a half-slip and a Chanel jacket, hair in curlers, fully made-up.

It's cursed, this place. Gabrielle cursed it. You can't blame her. Four years together and no proposal. Then I come along and, eighteen months later, bam. Not that it was that easy, but you could see how it looked to her. Like you played all your nickels, and the next person to sit down hits.

I remember the first time I saw Michael's flat. Bare rooms, dust balls, nail holes peppering the blank walls. Being a straight man, he had done nothing after she left except buy a new VCR and connect it to the wide-screen TV, which, his being a straight man, was the one thing he wouldn't part with.

Before she left, Gabrielle lingered for nine months, still living here and calling France every day to have long, tearful conversations with her three sisters, one of whom thought she should poison Michael, two who thought she could do better. Her mother felt that if he didn't own his own home by now he never would, and perhaps higher ground was indicated.

At the end of nine months Gabrielle touched him for first and last month's rent and a new Sealy Posturepedic, rolled everything up in the Oriental rugs, and sledded out like the Grinch. Luckily she'd found a reasonably priced south-of-Market indoor/outdoor loft space from which to date new, younger men and from which to phone Michael and threaten to kill him every five minutes. As Michael and I lay together in the dark trying to get used to each other naked, she called to whisper about homicide, but I knew she wouldn't. She was the gum on your shoe type, not the ha ha you're dead type.

She had long curly hair the color of redwood, and the thinnest waist I have ever seen. Green eyes, high Parisian accent, the entire catastrophe. I met her once at Juice World, when Michael and I were just friends. It was clear from her benign expression that she didn't consider me a threat. She looked at me like a fly on the other side of the glass. I have short brown hair and no waist; I go straight down from the armpits.

When they first broke up I felt sorry for her (this was when I felt sorry for anyone who couldn't be with Michael) and then she called me twenty times in a row one night at my apartment and hung up, and then I didn't anymore. I admire her stamina is how I feel now.

A few weeks later she called Michael to tell him that she had seen me again on Union Street, and that she was much prettier than I was. That may be true, I thought, and it may not be true. But today I threw out your shampoo.

Soon after she left, I moved in.

At length, I came across her markers. Unlike the lone for-gotten packing crate, there was clearly a method at work. Velvet evening bags, toothbrushes, Velcro ankle weights, a pink tampon case. Photographs of her blowing kisses into the camera; she was extremely photogenic, had once made the back cover of French *Vogue*. Sun hats, vegan cookbooks, a volume of Kahlil Gibran, in which she had highlighted key passages in yellow marker. A small clay cherub, which I smashed with a hammer. Then I prowled around like Jack Nicholson in *The Shining*, looking for something else of hers to break.

There is some progress. I no longer feel as if she is going to burst into the bedroom and spray us with gunfire.

This place is like a way station. I try to have the detached air that one has waiting for trains.

I don't know anyone who got someone fresh.

We're not speaking. Lines were drawn swiftly and wordlessly. He has the kitchen and the back office. I have the front of the flat, including the living room. I've set up an embassy in the bedroom.

Michael doesn't feel we need a professional photographer for the wedding. He feels snapshots taken by his friend who directs industrial videos are the way to go. Capture the moment, is how he put it. I would like someone named Kale from the SF Design Center who charges three thousand dollars. Capture the wedding, is how I put it. Hire a *photographer*.

Good things, I pointed out to Michael, cost money. Money is why we operate wheelbarrows in hell, I reminded him. We have money, I believe. Michael disagrees. To Michael, we are clinging with one fingernail to the lip of poverty's yaw, about to plummet into complete skid row destitution at the next unnecessary extravagance, like heat.

He's out there, right now, chopping onions. Chopping is helpful. I would like to chop. Now that he is, of course, I can't.

I hear a jar pop as it is twisted open. The marinated artichoke hearts I buy for salads. No silverware sounds, which means he's standing in the kitchen and eating them right out of the jar. A sharp report; he's uncorked a bottle of wine.

The television is switched on, the small Sony that gets the best picture in the house.

I want to watch television and drink wine and eat artichoke hearts. It seems more important than any principle I may have been hanging on to.

I want to have a good time, too. Or I would like to ruin it for him.

He's sleeping, covers spooled around him. I can just see his head above the pillow. Michael has what I call a stubborn neck, which means that from the rear it looks like his neck is as wide as his head. I observe once more how his hairline curves gently and comes to a point at his nape. In a crowd of necks, I'd know his right away. Still. I wish he were younger, because I am afraid he might die before me.

I wish he had never been married before, because he's already done everything with his first wife, Grace. He was thirty-one when they went on their honeymoon in Spain. I resent him being thirty-one with someone else. Deeply. Somehow he should have known, and saved himself for me. If he really loved me, he would have.

First wife, second wife. I will always be second. Even if his first wife dies, I don't move up the ladder. It's not like being an understudy. It's much more complicated. *Second.* It's so Nancy Kerrigan.

I told all this to Graham over lunch at Mario's Bohemian Cigar Store today, while we ate focaccia sandwiches. Graham said, "Why don't you just have his memory erased?"

Graham always has the best suggestions.

Phoebe, Michael's daughter, is thirteen. I haven't met

her. No one finds this unusual or even particularly a bad thing. The unspoken consensus is that it's cleaner this way. I wrapped her gift at Christmas and on her birthday; she doesn't know this. But I suspect Grace does. She knows Michael couldn't come up with those bows.

Michael sees Phoebe once a year, in Vermont, for two weeks during the summer.

Reuben says that "And they both lived happily ever after" are the most false and damaging words in the English language.

Michael talks to Graham about movies, they like each other despite the eighteen-year age difference. Michael sometimes telephones Graham to ask him about music when he's looking for something new. He is not ashamed to ask, What are the kids listening to? Whereas I surreptitiously copy down the CD titles from Graham's music collection, then buy them and act as if I knew all along.

Graham knows which CDs the kids are listening to. Graham knows because he knows actual kids, genuine nineteen-year-olds, some of whom he sleeps with.

Michael once recommended a film to Graham and said it was a feel-good movie.

"I don't want to feel good," Graham said.

Yesterday, Michael had to take the Cow to the vet on upper Fillmore, and it was a hundred dollars.

He has been spending a hundred dollars every day this month, he told me this morning, and is putting a stop to it.

He alluded to the ring, also. The ring which has sucked him dry.

I look down at my hand and the diamond dances and sparkles in the warm overhead light from our bedroom fixture. I laugh wickedly to myself, like the chambermaid who ripped off Scrooge's bed curtains. But only to myself. I realize that it is important to act as if I am not driving him to bankruptcy, a place I know with pretty fair certainty that I am headed.

Last night I clipped Safeway coupons. We are now going to save two dollars on Edna Valley Chardonnay.

Michael announces that today he is not leaving the house, so he won't have to spend another hundred dollars.

I'm losing weight. My watch is loose. The face keeps slipping around so I can't see the time. They say that happens when you get engaged, you dwindle. I feel uneasy. My soul may be contained in that extra pound. I could be pissing out my soul.

People I haven't seen in a while coo, as if I am a child who has completed a difficult task. It's clear that I have gained status in the society, being both newly engaged and thinner. My former self feels slighted. Was I that bad off? I was happy most of the time, I think. I don't remember. Yes I do. I was not so happy. But not *un*happy.

A dirty voice in my head suggests that this may be some kind of elaborate practical joke. I'll wake up alone in my old apartment, devils poking my thighs with pitchforks.

.   .   .

At four o'clock on Monday: Reuben. I sit down on the couch and say, "I don't think I have anything to say today."

"That's OK. I'll wait," he says.

A minute goes by. Then another. I become aware that I am paying for air. I try to conjure a worthy issue, not too big, not too small. Yet everything feels too complicated or embarrassing. Tomorrow is my father's birthday, but I'm not going to bring that up.

"I just don't have anything to talk about, I guess."

"Those are always the best sessions," he says. He settles back in his chair.

Another minute goes by. I shred Kleenex. I arrange the shredded Kleenex. I am not going to crack.

Then he says, "You ever heard of the gnostic gospels?"

I don't answer. I am thinking, Maybe he is too old to even be doing this.

He quotes, "'If you bring forth what is within you, what you bring forth will save you. If you do not bring forth what is within you, it will kill you.'"

There is no question now that I dislike Reuben, that he is senile. But just to shut him down, I say, "It's my father's birthday tomorrow."

He says nothing, waiting for me to go on. I sigh.

"That's an awfully big sigh, Eve."

I hate him beyond words now. It comes on in a big red wave. I wait for it to pass. Fuck you, I think. Fuck you and your whole sad profession.

A minute goes by. Finally, I say, "He was an alcoholic."

"Tell me about him," says Reuben.

I describe my father in a standardized speech, compressed into a few dozen words. Time, in therapy more than anywhere else, is money. Also, this way I don't have to think about him while I am talking. Not thinking about my father is a skill, the speech is part of this. It's the One-Minute Father.

I try as always to be entertaining and informative, yet nonpartisan. A Presbyterian minister turned bartender. His near-fatal accident in a Volkswagen when I was five. How he discovered himself and left home in 1968, when I was nine. His work in the Peace Corps. His strict religious upbringing, his astute sense of humor. His time in jail for drunk driving. How he marched with Martin Luther King to Selma; the dream he had to form his own progressive left-wing church. How he died with my stepmother, Leigh, on July 4, 1979, on a two-lane highway in Reno. How he wasn't driving, how they had stopped for ribs just before.

I wonder aloud to Reuben whether things would have been different if they'd had the half slab instead of the full slab. Baby back versus country style.

Reuben is not visibly amused, not by this or even by the name of the church my father proposed: Reality Church. I found it among some notes in my father's journal, the day my brother, Mark, and I went to the Filbert Street flat in San Francisco to clean out his belongings. He had also listed sermon topics.

Reuben wants to know everything I removed from my father and Leigh's flat. The Chinese lamp, the real Panama hat, the eyeglasses, and the journal. The fact that I counted his hats, that there were twenty-two; it all seems important to Reuben, everything I took with me that day.

Then after all this he leans back and says, "I gotta tell you, I'm not crazy about alcoholics."

I don't respond to this. He tilts his chair back even farther. I wonder if he will fall over.

Then he cocks both eyebrows, and says, "So how do you feel about tomorrow being his birthday?"

"I don't feel anything," I say. Which is the truth.

"Oh," Reuben says. "So that's what he took."

I tried to talk with my mother about the divorce once, without success. She shut me down instantly, like a camera lens snapping a photograph at night. After several separations, leaving my father behind involved an elaborate spell; my silence was part of that. Yet they excelled at divorce, remarrying right away, fixing up their own places. It was as though they had secretly taken correspondence courses. The whole country acquired this skill, seemingly through the air, during the late sixties.

Years later, when my brother, Mark, and I became teenagers, we lived downstairs from my mother and stepfather, segregated from the main part of the house. There was an intercom, they could tell us when to turn down the music. If we needed to send messages, we wrote on a blackboard near the upstairs back door, which was deadbolted. Deadbolted from their side, from the inside. There was no way in. Blackboard chalk is what we had. Allowances. An electric frying pan, a small refrigerator. Everything we needed.

I mention this time to Mark on the telephone today and he asks me if I remember being locked out of the downstairs, having forgotten my key. The main house upstairs was deadbolted, so I was then locked out completely, from all of the house. And what I did was I broke into the downstairs. I smashed the glass on the door to my room, and entered like a thief. It was never repaired. From then on there was a draft in my room, from the cardboard makeshift window: my punishment. I hadn't remembered any of this until now. With my brother's help I come back to myself at thirteen, crashing through the glass.

The Persian mystic poet Rumi says, "Keep looking at the bandaged place. That's where the light enters you."

The cherry-wood sleigh bed we ordered from the American Express catalog came at 5 to 5. I waited all day for it, developing a fairly serious relationship with a dispatcher named Hank. Then Michael came home and took out his electric drill and his large metal toolbox with the double-drawer set, and within an hour it was assembled. Ceremoniously, we tipped the box spring into it. Our mattress protruded like a dislocated bone above the shiny new cherry-wood frame. Wrong side rails. We stared at it. We turned it diagonally and sideways, captivated. It seemed like there must be some way to make it fit, if we thought about it long enough. We are educated people, from good schools.

Michael took the bed apart and stacked the frame in the narrow Victorian hallway. This gives us about a three-inch passage. I will have to take another day off for the men to come pick it up and then another day off to have them redeliver the right one. In the meantime we have only mattresses on the floor.

Michael poured himself a shot of vodka from the emergency freezer bottle, raised his glass in a toast, and said, "Now we know why it was only five hundred dollars."

I went into the bathroom and took a Valium. I have twenty-seven left, from the bottle of thirty that Reuben gave me. I can only have twenty-seven more bad things happen to me.

Saturday. Michael walks in this morning and says, "We're going to go to the zoo. That's what I've decided."

He likes primates; this is why he wants to go to the zoo. There's never been a better man, or one more strange. I ask him what he likes about monkeys, leaning back into my pillows and drinking coffee. Just enjoying his face.

"I like monkeys because they're more evolved forms of human beings," he says. "Their trunks are built for strength and their legs simply get them around. They're not hung up on legs, which are false gods." He pauses, considering. "Their bodies are covered with fur, so they have a really good look. You take an orangutan and when he raises his arm the hair drapes about a foot long like something Cher would wear.

"They're great improvisational comedians. Like, a gorilla will have a tractor tire in his left hand and suddenly he notices someone in the crowd who's pissing him off. And he drags the tire across the yard and he starts to beat a stick against a tree. He's handling this guy, but *he's still got the tire*. He hasn't let that go.

"They don't just go abruptly from one thing to the next, like we do."

"What else?" I ask.

"They're very direct. If they don't like you, they throw their feces at you. That's a freedom that we don't have."

He thinks a minute.

"That they even thought of that is cool.

"It's a big thought, it's a big idea. It's not like turning to a person and saying, 'You'll never amount to anything.'"

Michael has always wanted to own a monkey, ever since he was a small boy. When asked why, he replies, "It would be my best friend.

"When I was twelve I went to the monkey cage at the zoo and I did something, like I smoothed my hair, and the monkey copied me completely. He put me in my place. He showed me how affected I was as a human.

"Monkeys can lead you to other great discoveries," he says. "I always thought that you peel a banana from the top down. But you give a monkey a banana, and it splits it open from the side."

"What about the way they smell?" I ask.

"The cages are what smell," he explains. "They have to roam the house free. They probably need a separate mother-in-law apartment."

The other thing Michael loves is frogs. You even mention the word "frog," and he gets a silly look on his face, like he's just fallen in love.

"What's up with the frogs?" I say. Like Barbara Walters, I am prepared to ask the hard questions.

"You just have to look at one to know," he says dreamily.

There is a silence. I know we won't go to the zoo now; it has started to rain. But we can go there in our minds, through Michael's voice.

My father, Jack, who when I was little used to make up stories about Clarence the Clam and Wally the Whale, also had this ability. But then he lost it. He stopped going places in his mind. Or maybe the places he went he didn't want to tell about.

Jack was forty-two when he died; his second wife, Leigh, was thirty-five. When it happened, my mother and Don had already been married nine years. She swore that the night my father died, his spirit flew around knocking things over in her house. A picture flew off the wall; books fell out of the bookcase.

I remember her face as she wept into a huge brandy snifter, trying to fit her whole head into it, "Now I have no one to torture."

They met at Bible college, Johnson University. Bea and Jack. They fell in love, and since it was 1955, she quit school and they were married. He became a Presbyterian minister in Oakland, California; they had two children. In 1968 he grew a beard and left the church and my mother, moving with what seemed great relief across the bay to San Francisco to begin his new career in bartending. My brother, Mark, was eleven and I was two years younger.

After Jack moved out he had about a million apartments and jobs, mostly tending bar in fringe locations, collecting jokes late into the night. On our joint-custody weekends with him, my father took us to Giants games, packing his own cooler full of sangria. We went pee wee golfing and he ceremoniously sucked on his bota bag of Merlot at each hole, dancing a little swaying dance if he made it in below four strokes.

I loved Jack in a mythic and deeply suspicious way, but in the end I was freed. I can see clearly now. Death gives you a perfect little black frame, and after a few years, the picture develops.

My father was a drunk. The kind that never goes for help.

Beer with breakfast, Rolaids and aspirin throughout the day. Old at forty, prematurely gray and bloated, sweating out yesterday's scotch and always with a drink in his hand, *always*. Repeating himself and telling the same stories twice nightly, each time with a slightly different cadence, the accent on a different phrase. Although he had eschewed the church, he never lost the evangelical, the habit of drawing out his vowels and pausing for emphasis. The sense of rapture denied lingered around Jack; his midnight glass-in-hand silences spoke of fevered regret, a great joy misplaced.

In 1969 he took what would be his last trip to his highly religious father's house in Missouri. His father said, "Son, I understand you've strayed from the faith. I understand that.

"But how did you get so *far*?"

When I was twelve Jack claimed not to believe in God anymore. He would look down at me, lift his eyebrows way up into his Panama hat, and say, "There's no one up there," and then he would laugh a dry little laugh, thinking the secret thoughts of fathers. Down but not out.

In my mind I see him cruising in a long-finned green '64 Buick Le Sabre convertible, adjusting his hat so it won't fly off. I remember him driving my brother and me to the bus depot at twilight with no headlights on at the end of one of our weekends together, a Hamm's beer tucked between his legs on the car seat. I learned about the unsafety of men from him. It was a lie, but I learned it nonetheless.

His first job after the church was tending bar at Alioto's on Fisherman's Wharf and then the Tiddly Room at the Caravan Lodge. Then the Fog Cutter on the Embarcadero, which is now Pier 23, which he would have hated. Then the

Vieni-Vieni, on Colombus. He moved around a lot; he gathered no moss. Then on Independence Day 1979, he gathered a logging truck which knocked him eighty-five feet, and that was that.

In the final months, I rarely saw Jack. He was driving long shifts for Yellow Cab, barreling up and down the deep San Francisco streets with abandon; happy, alone, oblivious to the scream of brakes. Telling jokes and collecting jokes. He rolled on, away from bartending and toward his new career.

I wish I could be a fare in his cab. Take a ride up California Street and watch the seagulls circle the top of Nob Hill. I would ask him to describe what had happened to him. Not the accident. Before that.

At my wedding, there will be no one to give me away. I resent the implications of that whole gesture, the woman being transferred bodily from one man to the next. But I have been cheated out of it. I have been cheated out of objecting to it.

I was twenty when Jack died. My stepmother, Leigh, was thirty-five, just about my current age; my father was two years younger than Michael is now. I find these facts grotesque, unbelievable, and yet oddly comforting for Michael and me. We have passed an exit.

I recall that I once asked my father not to drink so much. I said that it upset Leigh, whom we adored.

He said, "Mind your own beeswax."

I don't remember our last conversation.

We never remember what is important, only what matters to us.

.   .   .

On the first night I met her, Leigh took off her shoe and threw it at her son Jason across the dinner table. He said something that upset her, and she took off her clog and pitched it at him. I thought this showed considerable zest. Leigh reacted to stimulus on a moment-to-moment basis. If shoes needed to be thrown, she threw them. You can't teach that.

She was always earning my admiration with exhibitions of fearlessness. Once at a party Leigh was talking to a small group of friends when Jack heard her say the word "prick," and he remarked on how he didn't like her saying it. He had an ugly sort of entitlement happening around his mouth as he did this. Leigh stopped and looked at him for a long moment as if gauging the distance between their bodies and the inherent wind factors, and then she leaned forward slightly and spoke clearly, three times in rapid succession.

"Prick. Prick. Prick."

Leigh nipped things in the bud, it was exciting to be around her. And Leigh could cook, could lay waste to whole kitchens. When she was done, the floor would be covered with onion skins and butter wrappers and crumbs; the sink would be coated with nutshells and potato peelings. Inexplicably there would be a hammer on the stove, standing on its head.

Leigh did something to spinach with garlic and olive oil that made it like silk. I'll never know what that was. She took that with her, along with a special chocolate mocha cake that elicited groans. People would travel from afar and they would stop at her kitchen on Chestnut Street for that cake. She served it with whipped cream. Because Leigh wasn't afraid of whipped cream the way most people were. She wouldn't whine about the calories and the butterfat. Leigh would just whip up a bowl of heavy cream and then she would place it by the cake pan and you'd walk in and there it would be. Whipped cream, with warm cake.

Leigh broke the spell of gloom for my brother and me. She did it with her cooking and her laugh. For Jack, too. She made it look easy, life. She made living seem natural. She loosened the vise of circumspection. She loosened the vise of self-consciousness. You found you could breathe in a room with Leigh. You took long, healing breaths.

It was Leigh who said, "Don't believe your own shit."

She taught me how to make spaghetti sauce and how to sing a high note when you added the tablespoon of sugar, which was Leigh's secret to ideal spaghetti sauce. That must have been one of the last times I saw her alive.

And then Leigh was gone. Death saw my father standing in the road and the logging truck making a beeline for him, and Death said, *Hmmm. Might as well save myself the trip.* And so, Leigh too. At least that's what I always assumed, that Jack was the primary target. I don't know why. I suppose I can't imagine Death fingering Leigh specifically, whereas my father had been courting Death for quite some time and had finally gotten its rapt attention.

They had been married only five years when the accident happened. She was standing beside him when the truck, loaded with wood and driven by a man named Grimes who was running behind schedule, hit them. They went together, hand in hand, into the unknown. Now they will always be married.

In a way, he was lucky.

December

The mystery was gone, but the amazement was just starting.

ANDY WARHOL

My friend Dusty, who grew up in Matador, Texas, and who has been clean and sober for six years, just called from his apartment in Manhattan. He told me that he is besotted with a recovering crack-addict alcoholic named Christian who just relapsed by smoking crack with a hustler, and then they were both arrested on Eighth Avenue and Dusty had to go bail him out while the hustler spat at him.

When I suggest there might be better men to obsess on, he says, "Sure, there are other fish in the sea, but I like these, floating here on top. They're easier to catch." Then he says, "Christian knows my old boyfriend George, too. George took Christian to Nantucket, and while George was sleeping, Christian stole his Rolex Oyster Perpetual watch and hitch-hiked back to the city and smoked it up. So I can't tell George about Christian."

Dusty sighs, exhaling on his Merit. He says, "It's so Gay *As the World Turns*."

I know he is trying so hard to make it, that it is especially hard in New York, where they're opening cushier new bars every second for people to rush into and drink themselves to death in, with sand-blasted bar stools and dishes of Kalamata olives and Moroccan trip-hop music. The problem is that Dusty is so crazy that he can't live anywhere but New York, so he's stuck trying to get around it, bars and all. He's like a forty-nine-year-old person in a wheelchair who has to be aware of every single foot of land. Always on the lookout for minor elevations and potholes.

I may have to fly out there and lock him in a closet, until this crackhead thing passes.

While we are on the phone, I peel an orange and it is moldy inside. When I tell Dusty, he makes a disgusted sound and says, "I hate fruit. Fruit and vegetables."

Then he admits that he probably doesn't even really want Christian. Too much trouble, he says. He says he wants to be someone's pet, so he doesn't have to worry about money anymore. He sighs and says, "I'm too old to be a pet now. Or else I'd have to find someone sixty-five-ish, in L.A. Someone who produced Adrienne Barbeau in the seventies and invested well.

"I wonder what she's doing now," he adds, with real interest. As always I can hear the steady hum of the QVC channel in the distance. Since Dusty gave up alcohol, he has cross-addicted to QVC.

Dusty was the recreation leader at our middle school, growing up. He has always been exactly like this; but the adults never knew, so we were allowed to be friends. And now the adults don't matter. Now we are the adults.

. . .

Michael and I picked out our wedding invitations, at a little store on Union Street. The salesgirl kept it light by chewing on a bran muffin and making personal calls throughout the interview. As we flipped through the books, Michael kept gravitating toward the more casual typefaces, the unadorned papers.

The first typeface he likes is plain and simple, no engraving or calligraphy.

"It just screams 'second marriage,' doesn't it?" I say to the salesgirl.

"Yes." She agrees.

"This is my first marriage," I explain to Michael, through her.

At length we choose a different typeface for the invitations, one Michael really likes. I agree, although the *S*'s look like meat hooks.

The whole invitation-ordering process makes me uneasy. The tiny awkward couch, the salesgirl and her huge endless crumbly muffin. The oversized sample books crowd me with choices, all of them unbelievably petty but nonetheless irrevocable and symbolic in some deep, unconsidered way. Everything says something about us as a couple. Even the envelopes. "The first impression," I am informed by the salesgirl.

Michael then tries to dissuade me from envelope lining. The one I like is a satiny alabaster. Forty-five dollars extra. I hold my ground. I feel that I have done enough, agreeing to the meat hooks. I don't want plain envelopes. I want the white go-go boots. Everyone else has them.

Finally we agree on everything else, including the invitation response cards. Flipping back through one of the books, we turn to a page filled with examples of pink monogrammed matchbooks that say "Patty and John, June 12, 1994."

"It's so New Jersey," I say to the salesgirl.

In the instant I say this, I know that she is from New Jersey. But by then, of course, it is too late.

Michael leaves his socks on the floor when he takes off his shoes after work. This used to be fine. But now a sock on the floor isn't just a sock on the floor. It's a sock on the floor for the rest of my life.

At night he undresses just at the edge of his side of the bed. In the morning, he steps nimbly over the discarded pants, shorts, and crumpled belt. He is finished with them; the movement between there and the hamper would impede his speed and efficiency. Besides, they magically disappear, these dirty clothes. The enchanted fairies come and take them away.

"I'm not your mother," I say. "I shouldn't have to pick up after you."

"Then don't," he says. "No one's making you."

"You are," I shout. "You are by not doing it yourself."

Insta-Shrew: Just add diamonds.

Michael went to the movies with Graham, something dark and independent. Afterward, they will go to Roosevelt's Tamale Parlor.

I didn't go to the movies with them; I told them I

felt ill. After they left, I danced a little jig by the refrigerator as I popped a beer and settled in for the evening to watch the *Daffy Marathon* on the Cartoon Network.

More and more we are both sneaking alone time. If we ever find a house, I look forward to having my own room. Maybe a wing.

It's the constant togetherness that chafes. No matter how much you love someone, you eventually reach the point where you feel like Kathleen Turner saying to Michael Douglas, Sometimes I just want to smash your face in.

This morning I put a piñata up in my office doorway. People came by to bash it with a mailing tube.

Then out of nowhere my boss, the Creative Director from L.A., appeared. He wore a black linen shirt with a Nehru collar. Baggy pleated black pants and pointy eelskin Bruno Magli shoes. His shoes reminded me of Howard Gossage, who once asked a woman where she got her shoes sharpened. He never visits my office; his fun alarm had gone off.

He stood in the doorway, fingering his goatee. Frowning.

He said, "When did you put this up?"

"Just now," I said. He smiled mildly, looking at the candy on the floor. Mentally considering whether to let me keep the piñata or not.

Finally, he picked up a piece of candy, looked at it, put it down, and said, "We must not be keeping you busy enough. That's all going to change soon."

The Creative Director from L.A. said no more. He had the power to insinuate and then move on.

I waited until everyone was at lunch, and then I took down the piñata. Swept up the candy, put it in a bowl. People in advertising will eat anything.

Had a long discussion with myself about taking another Valium, but didn't. I have to save them for emergencies, not just humiliations.

Michael gets a phone call from his mother, Ilene, tonight, at 11 p.m., which means it's 2 o'clock in Brooklyn. She never sleeps, Ilene. She seems, however, to know just when we are drifting off to sleep, and she telephones then.

Ilene tells Michael to wear a mask while gardening to ward against asthma and that fish are bad, all fish, not just big fish. She also is worried about mud slides. Michael explains that the Victorian we live in is built on bedrock. Ilene discusses botulism and how you can get it from fresh milk. How the elastic on your underwear rubbing against your bare skin can eventually give you skin cancer. She does all this within sixty seconds. It's in the pivot.

Michael says, "OK," "Yes," "All right," "Really?" and "OK," and "I'll keep that in mind." He says all of this in the calm voice of someone who has known for a long time that he is going to die of a brain tumor.

I enjoy listening to him talk to his mother, then it's something amusing that is happening to someone else, instead of something amusing that is happening to me, to which I have to respond. Other than her quarterly visits, I communicate with Ilene via cards and letters and the sending of Harry and David dried-fruit baskets three times a year, which is what she always asks for. She's very nonspecific when I ask how she's enjoyed them. I inquired about the figs once, and she just about broke a hip changing the subject. I think she hoards the fruit baskets. I imagine her placing them all in a room somewhere in her house, a room that someday Michael is going to have to clean out, which means I could potentially be asked to help.

I can easily envision Ilene stockpiling against some coming disaster, at which time she alone will be saved because she has dried fruit.

My brother, Mark, has offered to play the piano for our ceremony. He is thirty-eight years old and doesn't own a television or a microwave or an answering machine. If you call him, he either answers the phone in person or he isn't there. His car has manual windows.

Mark taught himself the piano at age ten and was playing Chopin nocturnes from memory at twenty; now he teaches children and adults piano for a living in Los Gatos, just outside Santa Cruz. He's one of the best people I know, and the only person I know who has never seen an episode of *Seinfeld*.

We go over to his house to hear some selections for the procession. After hearing them all and drinking two bottles of Chilean Merlot, we choose Handel's *Largo*.

His new librarian girlfriend sits silently by on the extra chair like a big cat, her black hair fanning around her face. Her eyes casually assess my brother as he plays. I instinctively don't trust her. I know that look. It's the I'm Waiting to See If Someone Better Comes Along look. I half expect her to start licking her hands to groom herself, but she doesn't. She just watches.

I want to say, I see you, bitch.

I just read the tiny, nine-point-type information sheet inside my Pill packet. Michael made me go on the Pill, is how I tell it to myself, but actually I did it to control my PMS, which it isn't doing. I still feel like Joan Crawford on steroids. I was so gratified when Beth told me she was PMSing once and got into a fight with her mother and wanted to pull over on the freeway, push her out of the car, and back over her.

I inspected the Pill brochure to see if there was any truth to the rumor of side effects. Upon inspection, nothing proved askance but an increased risk for sterility, high blood pressure, and cancer of the breast, cervix, and liver. Oh, and blood clots that fly swiftly to your brain.

When you pass thirty-five as a woman and your hormones start raging, they should just tell you, You get to be sick, or you get to take drugs that kill you. Then they could pass out magazines to flip through until you decide.

I call my friend Ray at his law firm in Dallas, where he moved after college and never moved back. People in high school used to hate Ray because he was muscular and good-looking and first-string quarterback, but he just kept on being those things. Then Ray stopped playing football and went to Stanford with me, also majoring in English with a straight B-minus average. We were nothing there together, which was kind of nice. Nobody hates you.

Ray says he just talked to Dusty. Dusty and Ray have been friends as long as Dusty and I have been friends. I ask Ray how Dusty is doing.

"Still gay," he says. Ray's been married twice and has twin sons.

Ray launches into an impromptu discussion about the upcoming holidays and religion. He says, "I only went to church because I loved my dad. It meant nothing to me."

Like mine, Ray's father was a minister, and unlike mine, his father still practices: Episcopalian.

"I believe all religion was a human creation to deal with suffering, back when everybody only lived to be twenty-three. They had to believe in something," he says. "When I heard about the Mormons, with the crickets and shit, I couldn't believe it.

"The Muslims are no better," he adds.

I wait for him to tell me about the Muslims. He does.

"It's all about some spaceship," he says in a confused voice. "And Allah arriving on the other side of the moon, along with some guys on camels."

There is a small pause. Ray receives an incoming business call from New York, which he summarily dismisses.

"I know it has something to do with the other side of the moon, camels, and some golden path. I mean if you just wrote up the unabridged version of that and plopped it down in front of one hundred people who'd never been introduced to any of it, they'd tell you: 'This is a loon case. This is a cult.'

"Look at the Catholics," he says. He's drawling now. "All those uniforms for everybody and the pope in a pointy white hat, saying not to use condoms and how women can't be priests.

"And there's a *bunch* of 'em, man."

Ray's wife is Catholic. He tells me she has recently

announced that she wants their two boys to be raised Catholic. Which is why I guess we're talking about all this; also because we both like to talk instead of doing what we're supposed to be doing, which is operating our wheelbarrows in hell. He continues, in his summation voice.

"I just want to say to all of these religions, What are you *talking* about? Just give me a shred of evidence.

"I mean, all we know for sure is, you go into the ground and worms eat you."

Right after I talk to Ray, I call Dusty. I can hear his television on in the background. I tell him I'm flirting with the idea of Judaism, after Michael and I are married.

Dusty says that nobody's doing Judaism anymore, that the new thing in New York is Buddhism, which he says is much more circa 2010.

"Christians were the eighties, Jews were the nineties, and now it's Buddhism."

I tell him about Ray's wife wanting their sons to be raised Catholic.

He sighs like he has just seen a hurt puppy.

"Catholicism is so sad. Very fifties."

He further informs me that Mormonism is the religion of repressed homosexuality . . . thus the polygamy. In a high falsetto, he says, "I *can't* be gay—just ask my wives!"

Dusty thinks that Paul Newman is gay, and Tom Cruise and John Travolta and Al Gore. Also Mister Rogers and the original Captain Kangaroo.

Then he says, "I have to go now. They're doing *Big Bold Gold* on QVC, and they don't do that very often."

Last night an argument. They come out of nowhere, like tornadoes.

Michael yelled, I cried. I took the ring off, which is my big move now. I don't just take it off; I take it off, put it in its box, and hand it back to him.

He put it in his pocket and went to the Lucky Penny twenty-four-hour coffee shop on Geary and ate a patty melt.

"Patty melts are good when you're mad," he said to me this morning. It was all he said. But he did hand the ring box back.

After he went to work, I looked inside the box to make sure the ring was there. Then I slipped it onto my third finger and called my best friend, Lana, in Albuquerque. Lana and I met in homeroom in seventh grade; we've known each other twenty-four years. Lana looks like Linda Hamilton and can crack every bone in her body.

"It was about chicken broth," I say. "We were out of chicken broth."

I hear her nod, from the teacher's lunchroom at the high school where she teaches drama. In the middle of my story she stops me and says, "Hold on . . .

"What's going on?" she screams at her students down the hall. I hear her suede-booted footsteps going toward them. I hear them scatter. In a minute she comes back to the phone and says in a normal voice, "Go ahead."

I tell Lana everything, which feels great because, for most people, I edit. Most people are definitely getting along on the Cliffs Notes.

It started when I was making a recipe, from Susan

Powter's cookbook, I told her. I started cooking and discovered that we were out of garlic.

I went into the living room and announced this to Michael, who was flopped out on the couch, watching the news. He snapped off the television, put on his coat, and walked to the corner store to buy garlic, with the air of a man about to donate bone marrow. He came home and threw the garlic down the hall, onto the kitchen table. Then he went back to the couch.

It goes without saying that I was never out of fresh garlic when I lived alone.

I got to the end of the recipe and went into the living room and said, "Guess what, we're out of chicken broth." He stood up and placed one fist on his hip, like the letter *P*.

"You should have read ahead in the recipe," he accused.

At that point, I did what I had to do: I implicated him in the missing broth. I said that last time I looked, we had plenty of broth. He must have used it up, I said, and not told anyone.

We both commenced shouting at the same time. It seemed we were no longer discussing chicken broth but who was going to get the final space in the lifeboat.

I kept saying, "Listen, it's no big deal, I just need some CHICKEN BROTH."

Then Michael went to the Lucky Penny and had a patty melt. I put everything away in the refrigerator and had a bowl of Grape Nuts.

When I tell Lana all of this, she describes how she and Raul fight over who is going to change Isabel's diaper, how he claims the baby doesn't need to be changed when her diaper is hanging to her ankles, stuffed. When her turds are literally skittering across the floor.

"They're that way," Lana says, brightly. Then she whispers in a demonic hush, "Spoiled."

This makes me feel better, more normal. Yet I suspect deep down that it is not all his fault. Mama's making the Shake 'n Bake, but I'm helping somehow.

One thing I know for certain, this is not about chicken broth. When I think of finding out what it is about, I want to weep with fatigue.

After my session with Reuben I bought six cans of chicken broth and three large heads of garlic. I know it's not that simple, but it feels good.

Reuben says he wishes everyone who gets married to have a good fighting marriage. He himself has a good fighting marriage, to another psychoanalyst whose name is Sheila. It's possible for me to believe in good, fighting marriages and also be very glad that he and his wife don't live upstairs. I think once you've heard your therapist shrieking over who ate the last banana, you're finished.

Michael's mother, Ilene, called last night, and I answered the phone, thinking it was Michael. Busted.

Ilene told me that women have to act like the man is smarter, even though he's not, and they have to act like the man is stronger, even though he's not.

She said I have to be nice to Michael, and patient. So he's told her about the arguments.

"You have to be nice to Michael." She said, "It's your job, as his wife." Ilene is not one to mince words. She doesn't mind conflict; it makes her feel more alive.

"I'm not his wife yet," I said. She ignores this. Like a tank, she is able to barrel over ground most lesser vehicles are slowed by.

"You have to make him happy, as a man."

I took a cleansing breath. Finally I said, "Yes, but it's hard making someone happy three hundred and sixty-five days a year."

"Well, you have to," she said. "Other*wise* . . ." Her voice trails off to indicate a terrible conclusion, which is understood to be unspeakable.

Then she was off, in a puff of orange smoke.

We're flying to Taos, for Lana's wedding to Raul.

Lana and I got engaged within two weeks of each other, this last fall. Both of us to men who've been divorced and have one child. Somehow without exactly planning it, we do everything together; except she and Raul had Isabel a year before they got engaged. We've been friends longer than we've been people; she's the sister I never had. The jackpot sibling.

Lana got engaged first. That's what triggered the ultimatum I gave to Michael over coffee. Lana and I had both been waiting for a long time, and then when she got hers, I wanted mine. Commitment-wise, things between Michael and me went instantly from Unresolved to Fucking Unacceptable.

When it happened, she called me before she even called her mother. I hung up the phone with her by pressing my finger on the flash button, and then I released the flash button and speed-dialed Michael at his office to relay the news.

"Raul just asked Lana to marry him."

That's all I said. But as everyone knows, it's not what you say. It's how you say it.

Now Michael's right here next to me, eating dry-roasted peanuts. Engaged to be married. Finished, in other words. Off the shelf. Whenever we hit turbulence, he holds my hand and squeezes. Not as if he is afraid, but as if he is just checking to see if I'm ripe.

It is tempting to believe that everything is going according to plan.

Lana's wedding was lovely; they lit luminarias and we looked out over the Taos valley, which was covered in snow. Her mother, Eleanor, gave her away, alone. A small altar held her father Richard's photograph in a silver frame, one where he is entertaining his grandchildren with jokes, his face white with cancer.

"Who gives this woman into this marriage?"

"Her father and I," Eleanor said.

Her voice broke only a little. She is brave, so we all pretended to be.

Isabel, their one-year-old, padded uncertainly down the aisle in tiny white slippers festooned with baby roses, chewing up the scenery. It seemed then as though that was the only good way, the sensible way. To have your baby and then get married.

Now that it's all over I worry that Raul isn't tall enough for Lana.

We used to make elaborate sundaes and name them after ourselves, with Frosted Flakes, raisins, coffee ice cream, and chocolate syrup. We went to school together every day on the same bus, which we constantly missed. She lived on my street, only down the block a little. If she walked in with John F. Kennedy Jr., I would find something to criticize. I'm that fucked up.

Back at work, sitting in my office, staring at Coit Tower. I am waiting for them to come for me: the account team. The men and women in Banana Republic suits and Ann Taylor outfits.

It's not paranoia. They will come for us, for Graham and me. We have just sold a television campaign, and we have only minutes of cool freedom left. The wheels have been set into motion; the onerous wheel of production turns. Hands reach out for us, the hands of middle management, the people who stop exciting things from happening. They will swoop, confident in their soft black cashmere V-neck sweaters. Creeping up to my office with good reasons to change the copy, mincing on thin-soled Italian shoes, like assassins. Their eyeglasses and shoes are always Italian. They work under the principle that if they can accessorize European, they can *be* European.

They point toward the storyboards with their best church faces. They know what the client wants. They know that in advance, possessing great psychic powers which they choose to use exclusively in the advertising community. They will come and decree that revisions are vital, large and sweeping triple bypass revisions. If Graham and I pretend they are not there, they retaliate. They want to be part of the process, so they run back to their offices and their computers and they produce something terrible. It is called electronic mail. "E-mail" to those more advanced.

In these electronic missives, the People Who Stop Exciting Things From Happening are able to write things they are afraid to say to your face—like, Oh we've moved the airdates up six weeks. We've added outdoor, two retail donuts, and a radio campaign to the overall mix. We've promised the client they can absolutely be on for their mother's birthday.

E-mails arrive hourly, like death threats. Paper-free memos fan across the agency in a gay electronic confetti of idiocy.

We told the client we had the power to turn back time.

This morning, the traffic manager blindsides me in the elevator. She is feral. If I squint just a little, she is a starved wolverine. She snarls and frets and talks about how we need final three-quarter-inch tape by the first. I am afraid and want to kill her with a stick. In a far-off corner of my mind I know I am in no real danger. In the animal kingdom I am superior, and she cannot hurt me. Her goal is to make me care about deadlines. Deadlines that the account people have created, absurd and garishly impossible Mad Hatter deadlines, deadlines that the account people have promised to the client.

And now they all converge in the halls about us; I can feel them. The wolverine, the producers, the account people with their traveling psychic fair, and the people from media. They are all oozing concern, manufacturing it constantly, in relentless shifts. They are ambulatory concern factories.

We made a bad mistake, Graham and I. We wrote a campaign that people understood. They will make sure that it is produced, now, to their exact specifications. And when it's all over, if it is successful, the Creative Director from L.A.

will take full credit for it. If it fails, he will distance himself from it.

It is a shameful occupation. We do it for the money.

More e-mails arrive on black poison-tipped arrows of circuitry. I hear the sound of them arriving, the gay little beep-beep that means the end of repose, of invisibility. I dare not open them all, yet the mailbox icon on my screen will blink like the timer on a hydrogen bomb until I do open them all. One by one.

It seems the media department has airdates for the campaign all arranged. They have Time bought. Now that Time has been bought and paid for, something must be placed into the Time. They will not go away until that Time is filled with an advertisement. Now that I grasp their terrible vision of the campaign, I am of course horrified that I ever thought of it in the first place. But it must be produced. Time has been bought. They will not consider thirty seconds of silent prayer to be a refreshing change of pace. My suggestion to have a homeless man recite *Desiderata* will not be considered.

I wonder why I needed to get here in the first place. Something about wanting to write something, anything, for a living. Something about being a *creative*, whatever that is. It all seems far, now that I'm in the forest of it. Now that I'm here, now that I see the trees themselves, I don't know if I like the trees. They seem sinister.

Life says, Tough shit. Those are your trees.

I stare at Coit Tower a little harder, milking it for all it is worth.

Michael says that the unadvertised eighth law to spiritual success is *Avoid confrontations within your own mind*.

"Consciousness is a burden," he says, imitating Deepak Chopra perfectly.

"If you think of your mind as a seething serpent, why would you walk toward it?"

It's 3 a.m. A man just went down the street, past our flat and toward the housing projects, pinwheeling his arms and shouting, "If I see Jesus, I SOCK his ass."

Christmas. Michael drove me to Point Bonita on his motorcycle, nestled in the Marin headlands, past the point where tourists dare to tread. An immaculate view of the Golden Gate Bridge, with wooden benches and sturdy BBQ grills. He was wearing the new Aerostitch motorcycle suit I gave him, which has black ballistic patches and counterintuitive zippers and cost seven hundred dollars.

"We could roast weenies," he said, demonstrating the hinged posts the grills rest on, which can turn against the wind and shield themselves. "We could bring some Polish sausages," he said, "and split open buns and toast them."

We sat by ourselves and drank a bottle of Newcastle ale and ate the package of Turtles I put in his stocking. I gave him two and ate one.

I praised the newfound site. I have learned not to let talent go unrecognized.

"Just keep steering the conversation back to them," is what my mother says. I will never liberate her and have almost stopped wanting to. Having survived the first quarter of my engagement, I now recognize her twenty-five-year marriage to my stepfather, Don, as something impossible and skilled, like spoon bending.

I had my first in-line roller-skating lesson today, on my new skates which Michael gave me for Christmas. He ran alongside, a human training wheel, as I slipped and slid my way down Presidio Street in front of our flat. We went back and forth, his hands clutched in mine.

"I've got you," he said. "You can't fall."

I have the sense of going back in time, and correcting things.

January

Hanging and marriage, you know, go by Destiny.

GEORGE FARQUHAR

Reuben said yesterday that there was something vague about me. I came in and said I was fine and that things were fine and he said, "Yes, but there's something." Then he frowned at my head, as though looking for where the bolts went.

I relayed the fact that, in ten months and seventeen days, I would be married. I described how I find this fact pleasing, in the abstract.

"What's alarming now," I said to him, "is whenever I notice anything about Michael, I hear the striking of a Chinese gong and the words *FOR THE REST OF YOUR LIFE* echo through my head."

"Like what?" he asked, far too interested.

"Like the way hair grows on his earlobes," I said. I wished I could clearly see Reuben's ears, but I couldn't. We just weren't ever going to get that close.

Then he said, "I notice that when you talk about your anxiety, you keep fiddling with your engagement ring."

I'm like, Jesus, old man, give me a break.

I denied everything, of course. Meanwhile, I'm sitting there thinking, When are you going to tell him about _____, and then my mind says, Oh no. That would really be bad. You can't tell him about how you and Michael have been fighting, how you sometimes look at him and he becomes a potato bug. You can't tell him how terrified you are of keeping up at work with the twenty-year-olds named Ian, of the Creative Director from L.A., of getting fired and becoming a person with good shoes and a blanket over your shoulder who walks around cradling a Styrofoam cup of coffee. You can't tell him that. That would make all of this real. It would make me a person with problems, who goes to see a therapist.

This goes on for the first forty-five minutes, then we work backward from there. By the last five minutes of the session I am talking very fast, like I'm doing speedballs. Talking about everything I've avoided. I can't make much progress, so I spill my guts.

In the "Traditions" column of *Modern Bride,* it says that on your wedding day you're supposed to have something old, something new, something borrowed, and something blue. The something old is supposed to be the garter from a happily married woman.

I know few happily married women. Those I do know don't wear garter belts. I store this away as information.

I decide my something old will be the ring charm I pulled out of Michael's friends Bill and Mia's wedding cake during the period when Michael and I were in the final throes of the Commitment Wars. We went to four weddings last summer, while I waited in vain for Michael to voluntarily propose. By the last one I couldn't breathe. A clubfoot, watching the women in white. Sobbing quietly and uncontrollably into Michael's handkerchief.

"I always cry at weddings," I said. Yes, but do you always hyperventilate? one may well have asked.

Mia had a white cake draped with tea roses, and inside were charms. I pulled one out, fastened onto a long white silk ribbon. It was a tiny engagement solitaire ring charm. I remember when I pulled it out of the cake, Mia, who looks like Deborah Kerr, said, "Don't show it to Michael, he'll have a stroke."

I did show it to him, and he stared at it like a blind man.

Dusty called to tell me he is buying a three-ton Chevy truck.

I said, "What are you going to do with a three-ton truck in Manhattan?"

"Drive it around," he says. He makes it sound like entering the Kingdom of Heaven.

"I have to fill the void," he says. "The void is really huge today."

I recognize that voice. It's his manic voice.

"Don't even think about another dog," I say.

Dusty has had five dogs, all of whom he ended up giving away. He lives in a studio apartment on Third Avenue. He's like a Satanist with those damn dogs.

"I'm on the other line with a credit broker," he says. "I have to call you back."

"No truck, Dusty," I say. "I disallow it."

"All right," he says. He sounds gleeful. I know he is lying.

"Go buy some penny candy instead," I say. "A big bag. Or, I know, go to Kmart."

They have a Kmart in the East Village now. It's doing blockbusters. Finally, people who live in New York City can get big jugs of Wisk.

"You can buy anything in Kmart," I say.

"What does Michael say?" he asks. Hoping for the stray electoral vote. He needs California and Michigan.

"I'm with the penny candy," Michael says.

"You guys are just perfect for each other," Dusty says, disgusted.

"Promise me you won't buy the truck," I say.

"All right," he says. "I love you. You're always so right."

"Bullshit," I say. "I'm watching you."

Received a memo today.

"... I want to ensure that we are casting *visible* Jamaicans and/or African-Americans in our advertising. My sense is that we don't cast obviously diverse talent in adequate numbers."

No more invisible people. Right.

The mistake is to read the memos, of course. It's just a way that crazy people can touch you. You really have to be like Ram Dass, who keeps a picture of Jesse Helms right next to his maharaja on his puja table, and says, "It's all perfect."

Meanwhile I shored up my courage and cracked the January issue. I am seriously behind on my *Modern Bride* checklist. I have practically nothing checked off.

I can feel failure gathering in a fat cloud around my head. I know I could apply myself and do well, but I don't see how it's going to prepare me for real life.

We were on the couch and Michael was stroking my face and he said, "There have been two women in my life with beautiful eyebrows. One was the Wicked Queen in *Snow White*. The other is you."

He went on to say that if the Wicked Queen were around today, the whole story might have been different, because she would have looked in her Magic Mirror and said, "If I got a little laser work around the jaw and eyelids, I might still be considered the Fairest in the Land."

Michael and I attended his boss's wedding last night. Seven hundred people, Grace Cathedral. It made the society page.

She wore Vera Wang, with the most wonderful satiny train and sculpted bow in back. It would have been better not to have seen this dress. This dress will do its best to ruin any dress I happen to end up with.

She glided down the aisle, which had long white tapered candles on the ends of all the pews. An angelic choir was singing into the high-ceilinged cathedral, which was draped with huge bouquets of French white tulips. We should definitely elope, I mused. Get the fuck out of Dodge.

The reception was at the Olympic Club. We waded through the sea of flat-faced white women with tiny noses and caved-in necks, holding aloft long flutes of Veuve Clicquot. In a side parlor, men smoked cigars with the satisfied expressions of sharks. Doorbell-like buttons lined the wall, to summon the expressionless Hispanic men who bore trays of fine brandy.

Willie Brown was there at the buffet, thronged by the flat-faced women. As I watched them fawn over him, I dipped a jumbo shrimp into blood-red sauce. I picked a pantied lamb chop off the buffet. There were whole roast beefs and turkeys, caviar, dim sum, two sushi bars, smoked salmon, dozens of pâtés. Pasta prepared as you waited, with a variety of sauces in silver boats.

"What's going to happen to all of this later?" I asked Michael as he surveyed the cheese assortment. In its leering abundance it looked not so much like food but nuclear waste. I wanted to make sure it would be properly disposed of.

Caterers, Michael soothed, often give away food to the homeless shelters. He was eating a plate of thinly sliced Norwegian lox as he said this, with mini-bagels.

It was hard to imagine that the beluga would make its way to the Mission, to the man on the street with skin the color of yams. Hard to imagine how exactly the yam man would benefit from the raw-oyster bar.

We left early. An Ethiopian valet brought my car around, I gave him five dollars. What I should have done was given him my car, and then had him run us both over. Death to the hypocrites.

Today the Creative Director from L.A. came by to tell Graham and me that our television campaign had tested well in the initial focus groups and would definitely be produced. He announced it dismissively, as though it were a prelude to something much, much bigger created by himself which he would at any moment reveal.

He was in my office for about five minutes, but wouldn't sit down. He methodically picked up things from my desk, glanced at them, and put them down again. I offered him a chair. He declined, examining a stapler. He of course had probably never used a stapler. He had people to staple for him. As I started to rise, he ran out. I thought of how kings have to have their heads higher than everyone else's.

When I left the building to go home, the Hostess pie and cake truck was out front, loading snack cakes into Kwick Mart. I looked to see if the driver was fat. He was.

Everyone is being their perfect selves.

I torture Michael when we're watching television; I take my diamond ring off and place it on his baby finger or his little toe. I put it on the Cow's tail. Michael hates this, so he finally grabs it away from me and jams it back on my ring finger.

This makes me feel like he's asking me all over again. A feeling that time can slide backward and forward, that we can afford to dawdle.

At 7 a.m. the alarm went off, on my side of the bed. I told Michael that I was taking a day trip to L.A. to attend the final focus groups for the new campaign: what Graham calls the FuckUs Groups. This is where, for fifty dollars apiece, people from all walks of life sit around eating free sandwiches and ripping the wings off the advertising we have created.

"I'm leaving for L.A.," I said.

Michael scowled, flopped over, and said, "You have to tell me the day before."

"Why?" I said.

"I need to prepare for your flying. I need to fly the plane with my mind."

I hear myself agreeing to this.

Back home, a Saturday. I went to my childhood friend Yvonne's baby shower in Pacific Heights. Immediately upon arrival I was cornered by a petite blond woman from Yvonne's office who'd just left her husband. When she heard I was engaged, she explained to me, in detail, how love dies. Smiling and hovering like Tinkerbell, she described how one day she just woke up and realized she didn't love her husband anymore. Her two-year-old son, she said, is living with her in Mill Valley.

Then she said I should read *The Road Less Traveled*.

Eventually I was saved by the appearance of an eggplant frittata. I moved toward it. I told her it was very nice to meet her. And thank you for killing my buzz.

I left early, making up a lie for the room. Yvonne understood, knowing my history of mental illness.

I walked alone down Washington Street. The maids were all leaving the Broadway mansions, walking to the bus stops, to crinkled American cars that don't fit in.

I hate showers. All those women in one place. Terrifying.

I wonder whom I can convince to throw me one.

I tell Reuben about the dream I had, where the back of my wedding dress has a big hole in the rear.

He said, "How did that make you feel?"

"Exposed," I said.

He nods, and says, "When the Navajo weave their blankets, they put a mistake in every one. Because nothing is perfect.

"A very smart people," he concludes, putting his feet up on a hassock, and crossing them at the ankles.

At work the person in the office next to me has been made a partner. His commercials consistently feature pouty-lipped Asian girls in midriff tops and lean yet muscular men with lizard eyes just like his.

We started at the same time, in this agency. Like, the same month.

And when I pass him in his new giant-sized office, with a wet bar and a black marble shower, I have to fucking *congratulate* him.

Last night I made Oprah's unfried spa recipe chicken. I have to make it every two weeks now. Michael insists. He feels it's part of his compensation package.

The addition of hot mango chutney made it even more diabolical. We each ate about five pieces.

I am no longer losing weight.

They had a catered cocktail party for the lizard man. Inside his new top-floor corner office is all-new furniture from Lim. The chairs have soft, faux zebra backs. One of those really expensive desks with the black trip wire and no drawers.

I comfort myself with the conviction that he is probably, way down deep inside, profoundly unhappy. I tell myself that he is secretly terrified, just skating on his luck. Because he knows that others possess a higher sense of originality and style, even though he is doing way better careerwise and everyone in the FuckUs Groups seems to love his work. On the *surface*.

I drink a single glass of champagne. I smile, feeling the burn. I can't get over the fact that the lizard man is winning.

It's the Chinese who say, Envy is an insult to the self.

I told Reuben how I wanted a raise and a promotion, how everybody is passing me on the ladder and how upset that makes me. I admitted that I was obsessed with ambition and money and getting recognized by the agency, how I wanted it all now. The desk with no drawers, everything.

Reuben crossed his long legs. Then he said, "You're spending all your time tending the outer garden, when what you need to do is tend the inner garden."

As for the raise and the recognition, he said that he felt all of that would probably happen. He waved his hands with a bored expression. Then he leaned forward and said, "But believing in yourself . . . that's the alchemist's gold."

He held up one bony finger like Merlin when he said it.

I woke up today to a feeling of movement in my veins. I decided I had to confront my boss. I decided I didn't care about the alchemist's gold. I'll get the false gold and then I'll U-turn back and get the alchemist's gold.

We went into the Creative Director from L.A.'s palatial office, Graham and I. The Creative Director from L.A. demanded to know why we felt we deserved more money. He stood up when he asked this. The Creative Director from L.A. is, naturally, quite tall. He stood up and looked out his office window. His huge, 360-degree bay-view window.

Then Graham mentioned the solicitous phone calls from other agencies we have been getting. The headhunters from New York.

At the mention of headhunters, he turned around. His face softened. His head tilted slightly forward; he donned the mask of someone who is listening, with regularly spaced meaningful nods. His eyes hooded over as he calculated how little he could get away with giving us.

I said, "Do we really have to go to New York to get what we deserve?"

I improvised, borrowing from movies I had seen where Jimmy Cagney rises up to conquer the world. *Headhunters from New York* became a key phrase in my speech, because, as the Creative Director from L.A. knows, perhaps one or two of the agencies there might like to steal us away, Graham and me. Soon he leaned across his oversized desk and said, "No, of course not, you're not going to New York."

If necessary, his flat black eyes suggested, we would be hobbled.

Now I feel soiled. This is how he got to be the Creative Director from L.A. With skillful ease he downplayed our successes, laid claim to our work, and undermined what shred of self-esteem we had managed to hold on to. God you have to love life.

I find myself getting back to basics, emotionally. Just

wishing he would go away. Struck by a large Muni bus, and then maybe dragged for a time. This makes me know how unevolved I am, and why I am being visited by this sort of karma. Additionally I've discovered that whenever you pray for someone to go away, the next one is worse.

Graham is my protector, the one who sits by me and says the hard things. He is the first man I ever had a true partnership with, before Michael. Although he is gay, I think of him as my trainer marriage.

As for the job, we actually have no other firm offers. There is no New York.

One of the managers in Michael's office is getting married in June, on Martha's Vineyard.

She woke up her fiancé the other night at 3 a.m. and told him that she felt she was making a mistake getting married. She said that, although she didn't want to hurt his feelings, she felt he was kind of an asshole. And that she had been seriously thinking of calling her ex-boyfriend and going to see him. Her fiancé told her to go to sleep and that they would talk about it in the morning.

They are still engaged.

February

I do desire we may be better strangers.

WILLIAM SHAKESPEARE, *AS YOU LIKE IT*

We're in an interesting period of growth. The relentlessly booming Chinese gong is creating increased paranoia and friction. Little things matter more now, because of the long-term implications of marriage. In fact, let me rephrase that: there are no little things.

Today Michael and I disagreed over whose turn it was to empty the dishwasher. At the top of our lungs. I went outside and climbed in my car. I was gunning it halfway down the block when I realized I had no place to go. I felt remiss for allowing people to grow up, get married, and move away.

There was a fantasy that the moment we got engaged, we would be invariably happy. That all the conflict we had up until this time had been about commitment, and that along with the commitment would come contentment. But lately I feel fatigued and resentful. I consider how I labored to put on this Great Woman act so he would ask me to marry him. For eighteen months he parried and stalled and danced around the maypole of matrimony. For eighteen months I was patient and dressed provocatively and entertained his friends and listened to him go on about Cormac McCarthy and about how he wished he lived in the forties so he could wear hats every day.

For eighteen months I made him soup and rubbed his neck and performed really sincere fellatio and now I'm tired. There's this backlash of confusion, now that it's finalized. Like, why did I have to do all this? And, given our respective ages, what took him so long? And even, sometimes, why did I want this? I've won, but what have I won?

The truth is that now that I've secured him I feel like I can really tear ass.

Also, whenever I bring up the wedding, Michael changes the subject. He lets me know this is not something he wants to discuss. I say "wedding" and right away he says "Uh-huh . . ." and gazes off into the middle distance. Not interested.

This is how he keeps change from happening, I see. He doesn't participate beyond the minimum. He bought the ring, almost dutifully it seems now. Establishing a price, following through, the insurance. But that's it.

It's as though he asked me and then ran back into his fort. As though asking me depleted all his energy, and nothing more can be expected of him for a long time.

I'm noticing some other disturbing qualities.

He has a habit of chewing with his mouth open when he's tired. He wears his cap half cocked on his head, like Forrest

Gump. And he always has toothpaste on his tee shirt when he comes to bed at night. He seems to have difficulty keeping things in his mouth. It is completely horrifying, and I am going to marry this man. Funny how those two elements can exist side by side. Assuming they can.

Last night there was a row because I wanted to eat in the dining room and he wanted to eat in the kitchen. He started yelling at me and I took off the ring and said, I'm not marrying you if you yell at me, because the semiprofessional basketball player used to yell at me and then try to strangle me, and now I can't stand to be yelled at. Michael made a small mean mouth and, before he stormed out the door to the corner bar, he turned around and said, very quietly, "Eve? You probably drove him to it. . . ." And that's when the red lights started flashing.

At around nine he came back and made up the couch for himself, at my request. When I went to bed, I retrieved him from the couch. This means, I suppose, that I still love him.

The semiprofessional basketball player was the worst mistake I ever made, but it is also the time in my life when I learned the most. I've heard the human brain will automatically block out unpleasant or traumatic events, but I don't find this to be the case. I remember it crisply, from beginning to end.

I had heard of him for years before we met; he was a minor jock celebrity at a different local high school we heard stories about. The urban, flat-ground school. I had heard from mutual friends how arrogant and difficult he was, even violent. He had, according to rumor, actually turned down the office of Homecoming King.

When I finally met him we had long graduated out of high school; it was at a Halloween party. He was tall and rangy and good-looking in a baleful, shiny way. He looked like a freshly oiled gun. He appeared as if no one would trifle with him, no woman mold him. His mouth was baby soft, curled into a small derisive O. His deep-set brown eyes were the soundless barrel of the gun.

The gauntlet had been thrown. I decided I would be the one to change him. Imagine how many women who decide this very same thing end up with tags on their toes and surprised expressions, two white marble irises looking up at a stranger in a mortician coat who doesn't care, who if anything feels mild disgust: another domestic dispute gone bad. Someone weak, is perhaps what they are thinking as they tidy up the body. Dumb unlucky broad. And you're dead by then; you can't answer back. You can't describe what happened, that it wasn't your fault, you had no idea it would escalate so dramatically. You can't explain how wrong this is for you, in particular. You can't tell him your verbal SAT scores. You dead, sugar. You *kilt*.

I was lucky. He laid hands on me many times, but the semiprofessional basketball player never killed me.

Why did I stay with him, is the question everyone asks.

I stayed with him because it didn't start out that way. For a long time, I stayed with him for the beginning.

In the beginning he was an asshole in a sexy, powerful way. He smoked in bed, drove too fast. After a period of feeling dead, of grieving for my father and Leigh, he made me feel alive. He took me out to karaoke bars and sushi din-

ners, to semiprofessional basketball games and award cere-
monies. He made me feel powerful in our little athletic-
event-fabricated world, second only, of course, to him.
When we walked into a room, heads turned. I stayed with
him because of the turning heads.

Then one night he pushed me down behind a restaurant
because I told him to shut up; I was wearing new boots and
they ripped. He had them repaired.

A few weeks later, I was driving us home from a party
because he'd had too much to drink. He accused me of
being a manipulative bitch and backhanded the side of my
head with a closed fist. I was driving on the freeway when he
did this.

The next day I had a purple semicircle behind my right
ear. I had long hair at the time; I brushed it forward over the
ears. I remember it was most important that no one else
know about it. My own well-being seemed a distant second to
that consideration. Then the next day the glassy, soothing
calm as I cried and he apologized, swore it would never happen again. This began the cycle. Everything one reads in
dime novels and helpful pamphlets. Yet inconceivably, it was
happening to me, a college graduate. Not even a state college, a university.

By then my self-esteem was one notch below pond scum.
I took full blame for the situation. I strapped it on like a lead
vest. I felt so ashamed, I couldn't move. Literally.

By that time we were living together, in his house. Breaking up would have meant packing my belongings into boxes,
arranging for a van, and moving out, leaving what had
become my home. All of which required action, delibera-
tion, assertiveness. I had lost all of that in the brawl. I had

become what he, during our increasingly frequent arguments, had named me: *fucking useless bitch.*

At that time I was a secretary, making a small salary. I had to get together the first and last months' rent plus security deposit before I could find my own place. So there I was watching the cycle escalate as I tried to scrape up moving money, and he was trying to stop my breathing.

Later I discovered that the primary reason women stay is not always, as many people believe, due to psychological factors. It is often about money. And yet, judiciously, not just the poor and uneducated, but the erudite and the rich. We are all free to crouch in closets, back braced against the door. The fulcrum, the commonality that exists across the board: our blanket dependence on men to get by, to feel good.

I had not changed the semiprofessional basketball player. I had only made him more of what he was. A boy whose own father had held him upside down out of an open twelve-story window when he was three.

After two years together he gave me a black eye while coming down off a cocaine spree. He rolled in at 5 a.m., the tires on his Jeep emitting a short scream in the driveway. I was waiting up for him on the couch, weeping. I told him how terribly he was acting, and this enraged him. I remember how his fist suddenly arced into the air, as if on its own volition, like in *The Hand.* "I'll kill you" is what he said.

"Why?" I asked, falling, kneeling on the floor like a devotee. Why will you kill me?

I still don't know. Would like to call him on the telephone and ask him, but won't. Still the visceral sense of having gotten away.

That morning as I looked in the mirror, my life surged up

to meet me. I could not camouflage this mark, it was not blue but really black and wound a circle around my whole left cheek and eye socket. I looked like the sad puppy in *Spanky and Our Gang*. There was no way to cover it up, to pretend it had not happened. If there had been a way, I would have.

The next day I moved into my mother's house. She never mentioned the eye.

There exists a sac of skin that distends when I'm tired, beneath my left eye. *Irreversible tissue damage.* Something stretched too far, which has come back changed. I've thought of having it surgically corrected. Michael swears it's unnoticeable, the tiny pouch of loose skin. Yet not long ago, seeing me stare critically into a mirror one morning after a late night, he offered to pay to have it removed with lasers.

I declined. I did not tell him that I need it, in some perverse way. A reminder that you can never, for any reason or length of time, no matter how much you love or believe you love, change someone.

That believing you can might end you.

My mother calls me at work, with news about her girlfriend Cheryl who works at Otis elevators.

"Cheryl's fourth marriage is breaking up," she reports.

"Why?" I ask. I need to know these things now.

"She moved a mirror in the bathroom and he won't talk to her."

I express interest.

"He just leaves notes. It's been nine days this time. The last time was seven days."

"What was the last time for?" I ask. I know she will know.

"The last time was for forgetting the bananas.

"I never liked him," she adds. "There was something wrong with his face."

I wait to see if she will tell me what was wrong with his face. She doesn't.

"I feel so bad for her. She said to me, 'Bea. This is my fourth marriage. How could I be so stupid?'"

I think, How easy, to be stupid. How almost mandatory. The more divorces I had, the more I'd need to try again. Like Scratch 'n Win.

"He won't go to counseling." My mother tsks. She feels everyone should be in counseling, except for, of course, her own self. Then she says, "Cheryl was crying. She told me, 'He says he doesn't need counseling. He says I'm insensitive to his needs.'"

"A mirror and bananas?" my mother says, to her.

As she tells me this, we both laugh. I have a flash of insight that this is what makes her marriage to my stepfather last. The laughing at what's terrible.

Don was a twenty-eight-year-old bachelor when my mother met him. They worked together at the *Tribune;* she was a proofreader and he ran the mailroom. My mother, Bea, was thirty-seven. My father had just left her for the fifth and apparently final time, to be with a sixteen-year-old-girl from Georgia named Pam who made great fritters. Don was just this very nice, quiet blond guy in the mailroom who was good with his hands, clever at fixing things. Nobody you'd notice from the surface, unless you were my mother and had been married for fourteen years to a charming, handsome man who'd never fixed anything except a drink.

My mother asked Don to help her with some small tasks

around the apartment where we lived after the divorce. One thing led to another, and before long they were married.

"All I can remember is she asked me to hang some lamps" is how he tells it.

I can hear the couple across the street yelling. They appear to loathe each other on a continual basis. They don't break for holidays or Sundays; in fact they target those times as festivals of hatred. I look outside and see them chasing each other out of their duplex, their necks straining with contempt as they scream away in their Volvos. It really is winter now. The trees are bare, which is why I can see so well out my window.

Upstairs, the crazy South African landlady and her husband have terrific rows. When she raises her voice she sounds like an angry cartoon crow. I feel doomed, surrounded by the bad marriages. It may be communicable, and they just don't know it yet.

This morning I planted primroses, which do well in a dark season. I placed them in small clay pots which the crazy South African landlady will undoubtedly move. She's always creeping down from her lair, tiptoeing down the back steps and moving our things around back there. Rearranging our recycling, reversing the mops in the broom rack. Lining our Halloween pumpkin with aluminum foil. She's pretty good at not getting caught.

I'll look out at dawn and see her hovering in a diaphanous nightgown and high-heeled marabou mules, totally nude underneath, pushing our birdbath across the deck.

. . .

It's getting worse.

There's this monster that has come out. It could be nerves, cold feet, or delusion. All I know is it's progressive since the day we got engaged.

It started over nothing. Literally nothing. We went to dinner before *Don Giovanni*.

One minute we were being seated and the next minute we were drinking our wine and then he ordered veal and then I mentioned calf fattening pens and then without apparent segue he said something about how controlling and dominating I am and soon we weren't talking. We were hissing.

And then Michael looked around and said, "Everyone else is having a good time. We are the only ones like this. The only ones."

When did he become cruel, I wondered. Thinking of what to say next to hurt him.

"Oh, so it's my fault?" I said. "You are so passive aggressive," I said, smiling. So that others wouldn't know we were fighting.

"God you're a bitch," he said.

"And you are an asshole," I said. Enunciating every syllable separately.

The waiter came. "Is everything all right?"

"Great," we said, in unison.

Once outside the restaurant, I announced, "You go to the opera alone, I'm taking the car."

"How will I get home?" he said.

"Take a cab," I said. We were standing next to an ATM, which gave this suggestion extra weight. I walked over to it and withdrew forty dollars. I pressed the buttons for Quick Cash. I shoved the money at him along with the ring, which I had removed in my fury. When he turned to go, I suddenly felt appalled, as though obedience were the real crime. I started to cry.

"I don't want to go alone," I said to his back.

This drives the monster away. Truth.

Michael turned around, a disgusted relief on his face.

"Give me back the ring," I said. I couldn't breathe.

He handed it back. It means more now, the ring. It has attached itself to my lungs.

The opera, then. We just endured, for three and a half hours. *Don Giovanni* is completely without joy. A story about a motherfucker, it seems to me now. The only good part is when the chasm of doom opens up and he falls in. And when after the third act, Michael asked, "Can we go home now?" I said, "No." Glaring at him in my strapless gown.

The monster was back. And the monster wanted to stay. The monster loves opera, it turns out. The longer and more lackluster, the better.

Eventually it was over and we trundled home, exhausted and bitter.

Now I'm thinking Michael looked handsome. The restaurant was lovely, with gold walls. We sat in the Dress Circle. I would like a do-over, but this is not possible, except in miniature golf.

Valentine's Day, a truce. We had lunch at Zuni Café and then went to Stowe Lake in Golden Gate Park. The swans were unnaturally beautiful. They mate for life.

I wish they could talk. I have questions.

. . .

I tell Reuben about the arguments. I also say that we have a lot of good times too, attending the National Cat Show and making fun of people or scrambling eggs together in the middle of the night to the strains of Stan Getz. I tell him that I still want to marry Michael, how even in the worst of moments at the core I never stop loving him or feeling safe with him. I say that I know he loves me and that we met for a reason, but that we're in some sort of sudden unexplained shit blizzard.

I confess to Reuben how sad I feel that Michael and I are not paralleling the engaged couple in the print ad for Tiffany's, all dressed up and twenty and hugging so tight you couldn't slide a pencil in between. These days we more closely resemble two morbid grouchy orangutans in a small cage at a testing facility.

My mother and Don drove up from Carmel and we all went to Sunday brunch at Mel's Diner on Lombard Street. My mother is glad we live here because it means she gets to get away from the small-tourist-town atmosphere of Carmel and into the slightly-bigger-tourist-town atmosphere of San Francisco. Michael's mother, Ilene, still prefers Brooklyn, as she did when she was married. Michael's father died of a heart attack when Michael was six, but she stayed on.

My mother and I got into a fight because they were an hour late. My mother and I have only had about ten fights our whole lives. Michael tried to smooth it over. He can't stand family conflict of any kind. Finding your father dead in the kitchen at six will do that for a boy.

We all ate pancakes and then they left and Michael and I watched *The X-Files*.

We don't talk lately. We eat dinner in front of the television.

Michael slept the entire night on the couch Monday night. Another first.

I made fun of the movie he was watching, *The Third Man*. I spoke during some windy dialogue, and he said, "Shut up."

"It's just a movie," I said. Actually I think what I said was, "It's just an idiotic movie."

Then he called me a cunt. I had never heard him use that word. I wondered what else was inside of him that he had not used.

I stared at him like he had grown horns.

This is not the man I met, I thought. This is some other man, doing a hateful yet incredibly skillful rendition of the man I met. A shape-shifter.

He went out with his friends and didn't come home until twelve-thirty. When he did, he glared at me like I was an erroneous bill, and went to sleep on the couch.

"GOOD," I shouted.

This morning Michael said he didn't know if he wanted to marry me.

I said, "You're kidding."

"No," he said. "I'm serious." He looked terrified.

"You don't want to marry me," I repeated. Maybe I had just heard him wrong. Now would be a good time for him to say so. I heard my voice go high and squeaky.

"Don't you love me anymore?"

"I don't know," he said.

"Is there someone else?" I asked.

We are reading directly from the script. It protects me, I think, from going completely insane. The script is good for that.

"No," he said.

He is lucky he said this. If he had said, Yes, there is someone else, I would have killed him; I'm not sure how. Or I would have torn all my hair out. Something.

"I'm sorry," he said.

"You're sorry," I said.

I wail and rock on the bed, grabbing on to the headboard. It is as if I am on a ship that has started to list. He doesn't touch me. He doesn't stroke my head like he normally does when I cry. He sits on his side of the bed and looks wooden. A sad forty-four-year-old Pinocchio.

After a long time I stop crying and just wander around the apartment. I am looking for something, exactly what is unclear. I will know it when I find it.

I walk back into the bedroom. He is still in the exact same position.

Strange calm.

"Why aren't you mad?" he asks.

"I'm not mad because this isn't happening," I say.

I stayed home from work, calling in sick.

At six, Michael came home. I was terrified he wouldn't. For the first time since I have known him, I wait at the window, watching for his white Honda sedan.

He says, "I'm afraid that we won't make it."

I stare at the fire in the fireplace. I can't seem to look away.

"Things are bad," he says.

"I know," I say. The monster has won. All hail the monster.

"I know how divorce is," he said. "What if we have children and then it doesn't work?" he says. "You don't know how terrible it is."

"That is not going to happen," I say. Dragging my eyes away from the flames.

I believe it. I will make him believe it. If necessary I will hypnotize him.

"We are meant to be together," I say.

He says nothing. We hug awkwardly, like strangers. He does not kiss me.

I feel like someone has taken my life away.

I talked to Reuben on the phone. I stopped every minute or so to cry. He waited in complete silence, as though a plane were passing overhead.

"This is a dark time," he said. "But Michael's a pretty solid citizen. My sense is that you two will get through it."

"What makes you think so?" I said. How do it know, as the joke goes.

"I just know," he said. "And I know something else, Eve."

"What?" I ask.

"There will be more dark times, after you're married," he said.

"Gee. Thanks a lot," I said. Nostradamus of Marin County.

"You're welcome," he said.

Then he gave me his home phone number.

I can't stand being here in the apartment while Michael is undecided. I need to retrench.

I am going to go to Bea's house in Carmel, two hundred miles away. I am going home to mother. And we aren't even married yet.

Once again I have managed to reach original and staggering new lows.

My mother sets me up in the spare room. All I can do is go flat and cry. A big failure, a big zero. A weeping eye.

I cannot imagine my life without Michael. I cannot imagine not getting married. I honestly feel I would have to leave the country.

For dinner, she brings me a small round plate of boneless skinless chicken stir-fry with rice. I look at it. It makes me sick. I can't stand the smell.

She is trying to give me something she thinks I will like. They would usually fry the chicken and mash potatoes with butter. They never cook this way. It makes me sadder, if such a thing is possible.

She says I have to eat. But I don't. I don't have to eat. No one does. Look at the magazines, I want to tell her.

My stomach is perfectly flat. I get a small pleasure from this. Maybe if I get thin enough, he will marry me.

I take four Excedrin P.M.'s and a cup of Kahlua and crawl into the sofa bed.

Michael now seems like a beautiful tropical island that I have been expelled from. I have forgotten all his faults and remember only his good side. Over and over again I remember how sweet he was at Mel's. How he made sure the waitress put the butter and syrup on the side, the way I like it. It was only two weeks ago. We had pancakes. Surely no one who is going to break up eats pancakes together with his fiancée's mother and her husband in a restaurant that plays fifties music on individual booth jukeboxes that still take a quarter for three plays. He even gave me a quarter. I don't remember what songs I played, which seems suddenly important. Had I played different songs, we'd still be together. What I believe is that any small detail once changed would revert us to normal.

I stare at my left eye in the mirror, at the irreversible tissue damage. Maybe it is working its dark charm. Perhaps everything that had seemed to be going my way will now begin to reverse. In the end I'll be back with the semi-professional basketball player, still a secretary, still the sad *Spanky and Our Gang* puppy with the black eye. I'll have taken to wearing long-sleeved blouses and dark glasses everywhere. We'll pass Michael on the street, but he won't recognize me in my huge dark glasses. He'll be back with Gabrielle; she'll look stunning and will have my ring on. It all seems possible. I'll die a spinster, a gaggle of cats sniffing my bloated corpse.

I think about suicide. Not the act of it, I know I can't do that. That would entail action, of which I am incapable. But I lie and close my eyes and concentrate on the blackness. What I would like is not to exist. Not to feel. To cease.

At 3 a.m. I wake up and think, This is ridiculous.

I throw on my clothes and barrel home in the pitch black amid truckers on the freeway. They are all going eighty. I go eighty-five. One tries to run me out of the fast lane. I roll down my window and flip him off.

I get home around dawn. I slide my key into the lock. I feel like a burglar.

What if he isn't there? whispers the monster.

But he is. He is twisted up in the sheets, a glass of seltzer by the bed. His face is white.

"I have a migraine," he says.

I drop my clothes and get into bed. We lie side by side, naked and holding hands. Then I rub his temples until his migraine goes away.

I can do that.

Today we went to the Sausalito art fair, and I saw a ceramic bowl with a toaster and the word HOME painted on it. Michael bought it for me. Driving home, twice I start to ask him if we are still getting married. But I am afraid. I feel like we're walking over a drawbridge made of dental floss.

Later we are in the kitchen. I walk to the table, sift through the mail. There is a bill from *Modern Bride* for my subscription.

I put in on top of the pile. I wait until he turns around and then I say, "Oh. My bill from *Modern Bride* came."

"Uh-huh," he says, looking straight at me.

Then he asks me if I want spaghetti for dinner. He is tying on an apron.

"Yes," I say. He turns back toward the stove. I touch the bill. It is pink, with black writing.

I sit down, write a check for twenty dollars, and seal the envelope.

Tonight Michael came home from working late and went straight to bed without brushing his teeth or checking the answering machine. He crawled into bed, waking me as his belt hit the floor, and he peeled his clothes off, kissing me at the same time as he threw his watch onto the nightstand and tore the strap of my nightgown lifting it over my head.

Afterward we both said I love you about ten times.

March

Graham decided he won't be my partner anymore. He's leaving advertising to tour the country in his lime-green convertible and film a documentary about street people. We've been together five years. He was telling the Creative Director from L.A. how he was leaving the agency, and I happened to be upstairs, walking by. That's how I found out.

I feel shocked. The wife who has been left while the husband goes off to find himself as she stays behind with two-year-olds and chocolate-smeared walls and ratty hair. *The last to know.* As I grow older, all the clichés come crackling to life.

So much for my trainer marriage.

Stayed home and cried for two days. Thank God for Michael. He is all that matters, I'm finding out. Interesting.

. . .

This morning the Creative Director from L.A. called me into his office. He took me aside, empathy on his face. He pulled his chair up next to mine, and slowly put on his Giorgio Armani glasses. As though he were a kindly father, about to read aloud to me.

He said, "Obviously, you're not leaving."

I inched my chair a little bit away from him.

"I don't think that's obvious at all," I said.

He waved his hand at the air, dismissive. Brushed his long blond hair back from his forehead. "We're going to be making you a group head, of course. That's all been taken care of. . . ."

I thought about how lonely and sad it was going to be without Graham. I opened my mouth and said, "Partner."

"Partner?" The Creative Director from L.A. blinked a little blink. There are only nine of those, even though the name of the agency is Silverbaum and Partners.

"Yes." I look out his huge bay-view window. I think of Graham's little sliver of a window.

"I think that would really make me happy," I said. Still looking out the window.

And that is how I became a partner.

As I was leaving, he still had on the kindly father-figure face.

He said, "Gideon tells me you're getting married?"

"Yes," I said. Gideon is his assistant, whom he makes pour his coffee and who secretly spits in it. "October nineteenth."

"That's great," he said.

He smiled, but it was wrong. Like seeing bits of your safari guide's clothes wedged between the lion's teeth.

Ate lunch at the newest overpriced downtown restaurant with sponge-painted yellow walls and tiny wooden bowls of sea salt at a table the size of a laser disk. My wise friend Jill (who wrote the Calgon . . . Take Me Away campaign) and I were commiserating over Graham's abandonment. I told her I felt depressed, that I had been assigned a new partner, but still felt bereft. She promised me that it would pass.

She said, "Nothing ever stays the same. That's the good news . . ."

She formed a tiny Mona Lisa smile.

". . . it's also the bad news."

Beth left her husband. It wasn't working out. She tried for nine years, which seems to me more than enough; even derogatory credit stops after that.

When she was twenty-three and first met Robert, whose mother used to make him sit naked on the radiator when he was bad, Robert said that he never wanted to have children. This was fine, at first. Then she discovered midway through the marriage that she wanted kids after all.

When Beth tried to talk to him about it, he said, "We had a deal." She said, "You're right. OK." A year or so went by; she started running. Casually at first and then in local marathons. She asked him again about the possibility of his reversing his decision.

He said, "What about our deal?"

Being a fair person, Beth nodded. A deal is a deal. She started running longer distances, getting up at five instead of six. Her periods ceased. Then, two years ago, in some sort of medical miracle, she became pregnant.

Robert was unenthusiastic. He said, "OK, but he's your responsibility." Beth was sure he would change his mind once the baby was born. But he never did. Every diaper was hers, every midnight feeding and ministration of justice.

After Max was born, they stopped having sex. That is also part of the deal.

Then yesterday, on her thirty-sixth birthday, she loaded the baby in the car, picked Robert up at his office at 6:10 as usual, told him she and Max were moving out to her sister's house in Bolinas, then drove away.

She had put her suitcase in the trunk beforehand. I don't worry about Beth.

I do however wish that people would at least stay together until the day after our wedding.

I was at the Marina library today and there was a woman about eighty years old, in navy-blue Converse skate shoes and a yellow rain slicker. I was at the *S*'s in fiction, when without preamble she said, "This Danielle Steel must write day and night. Rubbish."

I offer, "She lives up on Broadway, in a big white Victorian."

She answers without looking at me, as though we are old friends who need not look at each other. "Oh, yes. I'm sure it's very . . . pastel. Full of froufrou beds. God help us."

I thought about how people don't get old, not really. They are their absolute selves until the last second when they die and go somewhere else, leaving their body like a tire on the side of the road.

I want to ask her what she thinks about marriage or part-nerships in general. But I don't want to wreck the moment, which is as perfect a one as I am likely to get, today.

Came home to a hallway full of feathers. The Cow had had his way with a small sparrow who had the misfortune to fly into the apartment. There were feathers everywhere, and a tiny bird head in the center of the hallway. The Cow felt great about it, you could tell. He was sitting there like Muammar Qaddafi, preening himself.

Even though he was working late, I left it for Michael. He came in at eleven, picked the bird's head up with a paper towel, and then announced that feminism had a ways to go.

Clark, my newly assigned partner, is very excited to be work-ing with me. He will be my art director for the new television spot next month, and possibly beyond. We've awarded the job to a French production company in order to fulfill our specific conceptual vision for this creative project. It's called Work with a French Director, Get a Free Trip to France. Clark has spent time with Graham and me, so he under-stands the prime objectives.

Clark says France is fantastic. To Clark, everything is either fantastic or else it's crap. Clark has green hair and graduated from the Parsons School of Design, after growing up on a hog farm.

". . . 's crap," he'll say, dismissing Herb Ritts or Mathew Ralston, or sometimes even an entire state. He once said Pennsylvania was crap.

Or else, "Fantastic," as when he's gazing at a photocopy of a fried chicken menu that he has run through an old fax machine backward, and then overexposed and blown up to poster size, having billed all this to General Agency, the job number he refers to as the Black Hole.

When he wandered into my office today, Clark and I consulted the Eight Ball about the Creative Director from L.A., who just had a whole spread in a large trade magazine in which his picture is shown next to a lot of work other people did.

We ask the Eight Ball,

Will the Creative Director from L.A. go back to L.A.?

You may rely on it

Will the next guy be an even worse bastard who fires everyone and brings in his own people?

It is certain

"Fantastic," Clark says.

The Eight Ball is frighteningly accurate. But we can't use it too much, or it will lose its potency.

I begin to think, for approximately the millionth time in my life, that even though things haven't gone the way I planned, it's possible that I will be fine.

Last night at 2 a.m., a taxi drove up outside our window and let out its passengers. A second later, a man shouted, "I buy you a shot and you hit me in the face. Why you wanna do that?"

No response from the other party. I know, because I waited.

Today was Graham's last day. I don't know what to add to that.

I got through it pretty well. Wrote him a nice one-page letter, left it on his chair. He was out somewhere.

At the end of the day as I walked to the garage, I started choking, involuntarily, a dry little cough from way deep. I couldn't figure it out; I wanted to laugh. Then I let myself into my car and sobbed into my hands.

I notice that, as the wedding date approaches, some doors are opening and others are closing. I have no control.

Beth got a nice ten-page letter from her husband, soon to be ex. She read it to me over the phone. When they were married, he went days without speaking.

I listened to her as she read it through to the last page, as he spoke about his deep regrets, how he knew his innate damage had caused the destruction of their marriage. How he was cracked, like an ice tray. Beth was obviously trying not to cry, reading it like a newspaper article, but then at the end she just laughed for a long time and said, "Christ. Now I have to *think* about him."

Went to Graham's flat in Russian Hill for his Going out of Business party. He had orderly price tags on each item in his home. A lesbian art director got there before me and swooped on the best lamp. Though I arrived quite early, I hadn't counted on the lesbian art director factor.

I smoked cigarettes sitting out on the balcony with Jesus, who is Graham's dog and who did not have a price tag on him. I bought a small chest of drawers, painted with red roses. His friend Craig is going to take over the apartment, which makes me happy. Craig has a business card that says "Craig Debora Taylor, Opulent Superstar" on it, alongside a color photograph of him with sequins pasted on his head and full harlequin makeup.

Craig arrived around mdnight and announced excitedly that the optometrist had phoned; his red contact lenses were ready, and so were the black ones. When I left the party was in full swing. I never want to see things end.

When I went back to Graham's flat today, everything was white and bare. Graham said that after the drag queens arrived at 2 a.m., they pretty much cleaned it out. Then he gave me a brown paper bag of items that didn't get sold the night before. As I walked to the kitchen to get some water, I saw a long row of bags meticulously lined up, military style. He had a bag for each of his friends.

I looked inside my bag when I got home. My name was written across it, in Graham's perfectly square handwriting. Inside was a small gold tray that his father had brought back from Italy after World War II, a blue vase, and two books. One of them was *You Can't Go Home Again*.

There exists an angel in heaven whose one and only assignment is to fuck with me.

When we first became partners, working on regional

television ads at a small agency south of Market, his parents came out to visit, and I met his father. He sat through the whole lunch at Fringale and said almost nothing, just two ice-blue eyes buried in an old mountain face, while Graham's mother talked. I had forgotten he was there when suddenly he spoke, an unexpected, slicing truthful remark, tossed like diamonds on the table. And I realized that he had heard every word. Just like Graham. He waited, like a copperhead.

Graham's father had a seizure last year in his London home while we were both in Los Angeles on a Pringles Potato Chip shoot for their new product, Pringles Sour Cream n' Onion Lite. He had immediate and successful surgery, and then quietly and unexpectedly died. Before Graham could make it back.

On his trip across country, Graham will make his way to upstate New York, to see his mother, who lives there now and is sixty-nine.

"I want to see my mom," is what he says.

We look at each other for a moment, in the empty whiteness of his old life.

I nod, not saying anything. As always, a separate, more complete dialogue passes between us, in the space just above our heads.

This afternoon I saw Reuben. I told him about my elves dream, where I am flying with Graham.

Reuben is a Jungian; at the start of our sessions, whenever I hesitate for more than a few seconds, he asks me about my dreams and I have to tell him. It's either tell him the dreams or tell him the reality.

"In the dream," I tell him, "the elves had come and then we were able to fly. We flew for a long time."

Reuben asks me what I think it represents.

I say, "Ascending."

"What else?" he asks.

I fidget in my chair. All at once, I feel too tired to talk. But I tell him.

"Trying to do the best work I can. To keep going in the face of all the shit. Of which there's a lot."

"What else?"

"Magic. They represent the magic in life, that you can't know about."

He looks satisfied. Then he says, "There are two realms of importance in existence. There is the outer world and the inner world. In the outer world you do very well. In the inner world, I sense you may feel that you are a second-class citizen . . ."

This is as close as he has ever come to a diagnosis.

". . . it's my job to help you with the inner world . . ."

I think he is finished, when out of the silence he says, ". . . where the elves live."

Drinking coffee, I think about how Graham and I have the same car. Both Saabs, both procured when we did our first big television campaign.

I remember after the favorable review in *Adbuzz* came out Graham said, "You know what this means?" I looked at him blankly.

He said, "You ain't got to worry 'bout goin' hungry no mo'."

To celebrate, we bought cars. We didn't decide together;

we just both liked the same kind. Mine was black; his was white. He got his first, and had it painted from its original color to a bright green.

My license plate is special ordered. It reads KLUUNAD, which is a planet we invented.

Another art director once asked Graham, in front of me, if he knew what Kluunad meant. Graham looked at me. Graham frequently looked at me while he spoke to others.

"Kluunad is where we go sometimes . . . ," Graham said.

"You know, when you're away on a shoot and the phone rings for the wake-up call and it's 5 a.m. and you don't know where you are. That's Kluunad. . . ."

He continues to look at me. As if I don't already know. As if I am a conduit to some new, fourth person.

"Or when you call people and they ask 'Where are you?' and you're standing with a cellular phone in the desert, surrounded by production trucks, and you look around and say, 'I don't know.'"

"That's Kluunad."

Thinking of these things is magical to me. Graham and I were definitely on some very weird trip, for a special, limited time.

I knew nothing when I met Graham. He never seemed to notice. He just quietly taught me which directors were cool, which designers understood. He brought in *The Medium Is the Message* and Barbara Kruger's *Love for Sale* and Larry Clark and Howard Gossage and Jenny Holzer books.

Then we did that big television campaign for athletic shoes, twenty-five million. Television, print, billboards, radio, bus shelters, phone kiosks, postcards, buttons. All with Jasper Lyne the crazy British designer who drove an old school bus and who truly believed that Kluunad was a real place. And every day we'd go up to the top of the Filbert steps and drink Guiness and chain smoke and think of new headlines.

And then it came out and *Adbuzz* and the *Wall Street Journal* and *Newsweek* named it one of the ten best of the year. And somehow we won an Emmy, and began fielding calls from various newspapers and magazines for interviews, which is what we mostly did all day long. Work the power.

And that was it. There was nowhere else to go.

What comforts me mostly are the secrets. The fact that we got away with so much, a lot more than anyone will ever know. The trips to Paris, New York, New Mexico, London. The spa weeks in L.A., editing and going back to our beach-front rooms in Santa Monica and ordering popcorn shrimp and Pouilly-Fuissé. Expensing everything and exchanging blank taxi receipts like baseball cards.

They can never take Kluunad away. I made it up, the word. Kluunad. Two *U*'s. It was one of the first times I ever saw Graham laugh.

It may be that I said it just so that he would.

Coleman Barks, the poet, says perhaps that's what God is. The urge to laugh.

April

Great loves too, must be endured.

COCO CHANEL

Last week was Phoebe's birthday. She's fourteen now. Michael is in one of his low-grade depressions where he wanders around like Macbeth. His appetite is shot and after work he just sits around with a warm beer, murmuring to himself, "I don't get to watch her grow up.

"My fault," he says, staring at his nails.

I never noticed before how hard it is to deal with his depressions in addition to my own spiraling moods; now of course I hear the Chinese gong and *FOR THE REST OF YOUR LIFE* and I almost can't stand it. Suddenly he is not the person I thought he was. He is a much lesser person, shorter and sadder and infinitely more damaged.

I look at photographs from last month and he is seemingly the same Michael, so I don't know how this has happened. I can only hope that when I come home tonight the old Michael will be there, and the other one will be gone.

He's not getting better.

His weekly call to Phoebe went badly; she was watching television while they spoke, and when another call came in, she took it.

I tell him to call Phoebe again and tell her that he misses her, but he says, "She doesn't want to talk to me.

"She's dating," he says hollowly. I have no answer for that, nothing to mitigate the horror of that.

I go so far as to make brisket, but he doesn't eat it. He can't. His pants are beginning to hang on him, a white flag.

I consider copping some Prozac and mashing it into his toothpaste. What would it taste like? is the thing to worry about. Detection.

There should be a long poem devoted only to the names of antidepressant drugs; Lewis Carroll should write it.

Elavil, Prozac, Wellbutrin, Zoloft.

Zoloft sounds like a very wise wizard who once was tempted to go over to the dark side but never did. His coat would be purple, I think, and his long staff studded with amethyst. He'd have a bird. A white bird.

My friend Jill insists I am wrong.

Zoloft, she says, is a wizened old woman with a black velvet bag that closes with a golden cord and has stars and moons all over it. Her empty-headed daughter is Elavil, who always wears white and ballet slippers. Whose hair looks beautiful from a distance but is actually quite thin. Elavil powders her face with rice flour and is engaged to Prozac, a magician who performs for royalty in silver tights. They will never marry, says Jill. Tragedy will avert it.

Wellbutrin is a place just south of New Orleans. According to Jill.

I feel despondent and hopeless. I thought being engaged would transform me. Instead I feel inadequate, unsure, deeply tired, and as though I will certainly fail.

Most of them do fail. Sixty-eight percent. I know all the figures now.

No one talks about this feeling. I may be the only one who has ever felt it.

I used to dream about being married to Michael, how ideal it would be. Both of us serenely independent yet madly in love, supporting our meteoric careers with a steady stream of great sex and European vacations. This is not going to happen, I realize, with a sudden weariness. We're going to be like everyone else, lucky to survive without one of us murdering the other, like the farmer in Oregon who killed his wife with a frozen squirrel.

We haven't even gotten married yet, and already I can quite clearly ascertain what Morley Safer would call the burning issues, just waiting to be fanned. His messiness, my impulsiveness, his moodiness, who spends more money.

We haven't even gotten married yet, and already I feel I've been married for several years. Is this what engagement is like? Or do I have the trick engagement? The kind that only happens to people who should never get married in the first place.

Today at our session, Reuben said I can't expect marriage to be one long orgasm. But he pointed out that it was better than having no one and being alone.

Then he said, "Time's up."

After the first forty years of marriage, the divorce rate is very low. I read that this morning. It did not seem particularly to help.

I talked to Dusty today and he said that he is dating a new man whom he is trying to horrify with true stories from his past, including the rehab hospital story, the cold sore origin story, and the story about how when he was growing up his neighbor used to make his daughter and Dusty dry out their turds so he could read their fortunes.

Dusty says he doesn't want this new man to think he's just the boy next door.

Then he says it isn't working yet because the new man just seems fascinated by the stories and wants him to write them all down.

"I was hoping he'd run away so that I could begin to like him," he says.

"You are so very unwell," I say.

In the background I can hear a woman with an intimate, deep voice selling solid perfume. Only two thousand left.

"This is *solid* perfume," she explains. "This is a treat."

"It's Tova," Dusty says. "Ernest Borgnine's wife."

Out of all the QVC hosts, Kathy Levine is Dusty's favorite. He also has a secret crush on Dan Hughes, who is the morning host and also the race-car host. Dusty has his own Q Number, which he has memorized. He knows perhaps a little more than he should about the hosts, frequently watching all night long and then sleeping in until three or four the next day. Yet all in all, it's probably better than waking up in jail, still drunk and swathed in urine-soaked pants, his last memory that of being carried out of a bar weeping. Probably.

"I adore Tova," Dusty says.

Modern Bride keeps coming: huge, wrapped in thick plastic. Covers resplendent with lace-veiled twenty-year-old blonds whose fathers are international bankers. Whose fathers are alive and writing checks in their mahogany studies, their boundless joy and confidence suggests.

"How much do you need?" they ask, over horn-rimmed half glasses.

None of these cover girls has ever buried anyone. They have never been stood up or hit or awoken with blood on their pillow from too much cocaine. They live size-2 lives of constant love and laughter. Their parents are still together; they hold hands and take long leisurely vacations where no one drinks too much or raises their voice.

At their large well-organized weddings, the *Modern Bride* women dance the first dance with their father. They both cry.

I broke down and called Reuben, using the home number. I needed to talk to someone about Michael's depression, which is making me feel not just helpless and sad, but depressed. And something else: rage. I think Reuben will be shocked, but he isn't.

People are never shocked.

He said that it was fine if I wanted to comfort Michael, and fine if I didn't. That actually by comforting him, I might be derailing him from the work he needs to do.

This feels like permission to be a heartless bitch. I run with it.

You go through sudden periods where you change your mind; you think, No, not him.

Husbands should be at least six feet two inches tall, you think. They should be thirty-five years old forever, and they should have thick dark hair and black Izod shirts and a pilot's license. They should never get depressed, providing emotional bedrock not just some of the time but always.

And he knows you're doubting him, and then he gets even smaller until he looks like a midget. A sideshow freak. A man without legs on a skateboard dolly in front of Macy's.

Then you pull out of it, you look at him again. And he's two inches taller than you are, as he has been all along, and it's fine again.

I also think about death more, now.

I used to focus on Michael's death, since he's older than I am. But now I begin to see my own mortality, winking from behind the folds of lace. Maybe that's why I am stalling on finding the wedding dress. If I don't get married, I'll never move on, and then I will never die. I can just date forever and stay young. No one who's old dates.

I search for loopholes.

Reuben nails my fantasies every time, with iron rods of reality. He asserts that I am going to die, but probably not for a while, and that maybe I should try getting married and having a life first. He's seventy and knows things, which is why I go to him. But it's sad to leave my romantic illusions at the door of this passage. Although false and destructive and useless, they've been tremendous company.

We were taking a walk around the block when Michael said he was a good value.

"Sure I'm depressed now," he said, "but don't forget what a good value I am."

"Why?" I asked. I wanted him to sell me.

"I'm smart, I'm funny, I'm good-looking, and I make more money than you do."

"Not by much," I say. I am closing the gap. Coming in hard on the outside.

It's lifting.

This morning, immediately upon waking, Michael said, "You know who has really nice lips? Mr. Potato Head.

"They're his best feature," he said.

He says something like this and keeps me from giving up on love, which is so hard and demanding and tricky. He says something like this and keeps me from leaving. Leaving is what I am good at. Leaving and driving people away.

When I first knew him, he once turned to me and said, "If I had to choose only one fabric, it would be rayon."

The honeymoon is planned. Tickets to Paris have been procured, using up all of Michael's Delta frequent-flier miles, which he didn't even know he had. They would have just expired quietly in his desk drawer, had I not ferreted them out. We are going to fly business class, 150,000 miles for both tickets. I'm stunned that Gabrielle didn't get to them earlier; they had somehow slipped through a crack in the system.

I read in a guidebook that the Hôtel Panthéon in the Latin Quarter has the perfect room for honeymooners, with a canopy bed and a view, all for less than two hundred dollars a night including breakfast. Room 44. I send a fax, they send one back, and it's ours.

This is tremendous. It is absolutely nothing like planning a wedding.

I am spooning with him, on top of the bed. It's almost noon, and neither one of us has gotten up.

Michael is reading *The Tailor of Panama*, by John Le Carré. He turns a page and cocks one eye at me, as though I am slightly dangerous and must be watched.

"One of the greatest living British writers," he says. "Any literary critic will tell you that."

"Do you love me?" I ask.

"Uh-huh."

"How much?" I ask.

"This much," he says, holding his thumb and forefinger about half an inch apart.

As I was packing to leave for a weeklong business trip to L.A. this morning, I heard Michael in the shower, singing "Do Nothing till You Hear from Me," in an above-average Louis Armstrong.

His depression is completely gone. It may be that I am a carrier.

Then as I was boarding the United shuttle, I started to notice that the plane was filled exclusively with men. Young men. There were about fifty of them, uniformly attractive, freshly showered. They all looked like Matt LeBlanc. It occurred to me that now I could never go out with any of them. The option to make eye contact and exchange phone numbers was no longer available to me. It felt as though my checkbook were missing.

I sat alone in their midst, looking about. Just me and the Matt LeBlancs, hurtling through the clouds. Naked under our clothes.

What I do is open up the hotel mini-bar corkscrew and, using the small knife, carve a tiny slit into the bottom of the cellophane bag of jumbo cashews and slide half a dozen out. I then replace the bag on the black lacquered tray.

I do this out of self-defense, to avoid the four-pack of Nutter Butter cookies, which are screaming out to me from behind their orange foil wrapper.

This morning I drove to the Rose Street clown in Venice Beach, near Main Street. I needed to look at it. It's a giant fifty-foot bearded drag queen clown on pointe, perched at the top of a building that has never been occupied, as far as I know.

What I thought was that clowns were all different: some were big and flashy, and some were medium sized and sad, and some were fat and smelled like vodka, but they each had an odd beauty. Each clown was impeccable. On some level you were always glad to see them.

I resolve not to evaluate constantly; nothing has to have a reason for being. Like that clown. What's he *doing* up there?

If that clown can be there, then I can be here.

We've been together two years today. On our first date we went to the Hillcrest Bar and Grill on Fillmore Street and ate turkey burgers with curly fries. It became our favorite place to just sit and talk. The bar was a sea of enormous comfy chairs. We held all our important negotiations there. Those were the curly fry days.

They closed down the Hillcrest, about a day after we got engaged. There are no more curly fries anywhere that I know of. You can't get them.

It's impressive how God attends to the details.

I was flying home from L.A. and all of a sudden I looked out at the clouds, and I realized, Jesus we are really flying, and it was the most wonderful and miraculous thing, and about a minute later the feelings of anxiety and panic began.

I feel the same way about marriage, today.

· · ·

My mother was driving down Highway 1 behind a big pickup truck yesterday, and a pig fell out of it. She veered out of the way just in time. The pig rolled a few times, shook itself off, and went to the shoulder of the highway, where it began rooting in the grass.

She accelerated and pulled up alongside the pickup truck and yelled at the driver, "You dropped your pig!" He looked at her for a few seconds with a stunned expression, and then floored it. Thinking she was just another crazy driver, I guess. Somewhere in Monterey, a pig wanders free.

This is a good story. It has a beginning, a middle, and an end. Unlike my life, it is not really important to know what happens next.

When he woke up this morning, Michael couldn't remember where he had parked his car last night. I asked him if he had been drinking. "I had one drink," he said. He raised his voice a little when he said it.

We drove around, me in my pajamas, looking. After ten minutes he had given it up for towed, stolen, or completely disappeared. He seemed convinced that it had been spat like a watermelon seed out of the linear universe. "I can't afford a new car," he said, balling his fists in panic. He can, but I didn't say so. I took a last pass at Washington Street and found it, a white Honda cunningly tucked behind a PG&E truck. He got in and drove off to work; he goes to his office at eight and I get to mine around ten.

This was one of the times when I stay calm and he goes insane. We rotate.

As I got to work I saw the homeless man Graham calls the Ex–Creative Director, sitting on the park bench near the water fountain, running one hand backward through his dirty hair, basking in the sun. He is wearing Kenneth Cole shoes, an unconstructed jacket, and greasy black tuxedo pants. I never see him with a bag of cans or a shopping cart; he always has fresh coffee. I have never seen him beg. He survives, I imagine, by persuasion.

I wonder if he was ever married. I wonder if there is a Mrs. Ex–Creative Director.

I fainted yesterday, in front of Whole Foods.

Around three o'clock, after I saw Reuben, I stopped at Whole Foods, as I always do. Right away, next to the Japanese eggplant, I started to feel dizzy. I left the store and headed to the parking lot, with great determination. The idea was that I would make it to my car and sit for a while before I drove home. One minute I was leaving the store and making this plan, and the next minute the white dots appeared and then they all held hands, and I crashed.

When I came to, I was stretched out on the asphalt, lodged between two parked cars. Nice, I thought. Private. My shoes were placed side by side at my feet; my jacket was neatly folded next to me. All of this I found fascinating.

Five or six out-of-focus faces looked down at me with concern. The base of my skull was cradled by a strange kind man. Because of his position above and behind my head, I could not see his face but just heard his voice. I liked this man, and the man at my feet who had removed my shoes, and the bag boy who had brought orange juice. It was possible that I loved them.

He spoke clearly and distinctly, holding my skull off the pavement with tenderness. He asked me questions.

"Is there anything we need to know . . . ? Is there anything you need to tell us?"

I'm getting married, I thought.

I explained that I had just fainted is all; it's happened before. Ever since I was little. They nodded slowly, as if trying to remember.

I held the straw and drank the juice. I rubbed my face, where a lump was forming. My arm hurts; the knees of my pants are torn. I begin to hope no one I know sees me. Self-consciousness wades back in. The kind man asks me if I can sit up. I can. I make a joke; they all laugh. With regret I realize I have come back. I am entertaining again. Soon I will have to get up, get in my car, and drive home. To get away from what I have created, which I see now is a Scene.

A second man, who had been running the Save the Rainforest booth next to the open-air crenshaw melon display, reaches out and takes my pulse without comment. He announces that my spleen is out of whack. He hands me his card: Jon Berkhald. Shiatsu Massage and Nutritional Counseling.

"Did you have a hard day?" Jon asks.

Jon wants to solve me; I can tell. He doesn't seem to understand that this is not me fainting; this is a documentary of me fainting.

At my two o'clock session with Reuben, I'd admitted that I didn't have any motivation or interest to deal with my family or Michael's anymore. They seemed like pleasant and defective strangers.

And now the strangers seem like family, as I lie on the ground. Perhaps this is my new family, I thought, conveniently located next to the crenshaws.

Reuben had said, "You are about to take a husband. This is the biggest passage you can make, other than birth and death."

"I know," I said. Then I drove to Whole Foods and passed out.

May

I don't have time every day to put on make up.
I need that time to clean my rifle.

HENRIETTE MANTEL

According to the lingerie department at Nordstrom, the Top-Ten Bridal Essentials, in this order, are:

1. A blue garter to keep
2. Another to throw
3. Bustier
4. Alluring chemise and robe
5. Captivating gown and robe
6. Lacy bra and panty/matching garter and stockings
7. Silk camisole and slip
8. Teddies
9. Silk pajamas
10. Forever New

Forever New is Nordstrom's own brand of granulated fine-washables soak. Five dollars for an eight-ounce jar; I buy two but no lingerie.

The top-ten list is inscribed on a placard at the lingerie counter. I read the whole list, and then I think, They forgot Valium. A woman standing near me laughs, a short burst. Her ten-year-old daughter looks scornful. I have said it out loud.

Five months and twelve days until the wedding.

What nobody tells you about getting engaged is he asks you and you're delirious for about two days and then it tapers. He asks you and you're running around telling grocery clerks and ordering subscriptions to bride magazines and discussing prong settings versus suspension settings, and then after two days this ebullience passes. And instead of looking ahead you are suddenly struck by everything you are leaving behind.

He asks you and two days go by and you haven't even gotten the ring yet before women, mostly big scary already married women with perfect manicures, start asking specific questions about your wedding, and it is then you realize it is no longer conceptual; you have the whole wedding to plan and from that moment on the pressure builds. And every time you talk to your mother she grills you about caterers and flowers and whose name is going first on the invitations. Efficient shop clerks whip out calendars and show you how little time you have left, actually. How it's a lot sooner than you think, the wedding.

You could say, Oh we're getting married in fifty years,

and they would arch their eyebrows and say in a lilting voice, It's sooner than you think.

A warm night, the scent of wet leaves sidling in the open window. We are in bed with our laptop computers. It's the new sex.

Michael is surfing the Internet. I feel very close to him, as though he were my right leg, or an eye.

Out of a clear silence he recites, "Omaha Steaks.

"Four for thirty-nine dollars and eighty-five cents, with six free hamburgers."

"How much is that each?" he asks, beginning to calculate the enormity of it.

A considering pause.

"Six free hamburgers . . . like that makes up for it."

I don't answer. My not answering in fact seems to fuel the whole discussion and enliven it.

A minute later, just when I think he's moved on, he poses this question to the imagined audience, whom it is his duty to enlighten.

"Have you paid ten dollars apiece for a steak yet?"

Then, "Might as well go to Alfred's," he says.

Ah. The epilogue I had hoped for. Alfred's steak house near the Broadway tunnel, featuring valet parking. Extreme old San Francisco bordello, full of mafioso types and Italian women with thick eyeliner and secretive faces. We are going to go there sometime soon, now, because of this. We will go there and eat bloody steaks and gigantic potatoes with everything on them. We will do all of this before we get married and have a baby and our lives end.

Yesterday there was a company-wide electronic memo about me. I was formally promoted. So it's official, although I wouldn't be surprised to be led into an empty garage and be shot in the back of the head like Joe Pesci in a Scorsese film.

Reading the e-mail, I felt almost nothing. I was frankly expecting it to usher in a new phase of personal power and self-esteem.

Today people at work have been stopping by my office to congratulate me. John Hoberger, a veteran agency producer whom we secretly call The Hoe, said, "You know what it is? It's respect." Then he said, "You deserve it."

I have to admit, that felt pretty good.

No one has figured out that I am an impostor yet. Only a matter of time before they find out. Then this whole charade will be over, thank God.

Last night in my mind I formed MAJM: Middle-Aged Jewish Men, a support group for middle-aged Jewish men and their non-Jewish partners. The former would have a forum in which to gripe about HMOs and the way the airlines are run and how you can't find anything good except in New York. They could renew their vows never to buy retail unless completely unavoidable, and then afterward, we of the shiksa would also have a chance to share experiences and touch base with our own kind, eating things with mayonnaise and acting carefree. Sticking forks into toasters and improperly hanging pictures.

When I met Michael I was thrilled to be finding a MAJM.

But I didn't know the whole story then. I only knew him as good MAJM, the wise funny great cook with the sexy reading glasses who genuinely likes women and understands fabric. The MAJM who won't let you buy second best, what he dismisses with a wave and the magical word *chazzerai*. I wanted the sophisticated MAJM, the well-dressed breezy professional *New York Times* MAJM. I honestly thought that's what I was getting. Not the neurotic madman who stalks salmonella, who has to rush home if there's a raw tomato in the car.

Sometimes I just want to say, "Wait a minute. I didn't order all this."

"It comes with," the representative from MAJM would explain.

There was a hummingbird outside our window, so we watched it for a while. Michael had just brought me my coffee. He has done this since the beginning. He used to fix me toast or breakfast, too. We are down to just coffee.

"Hummingbirds," he tells me, "have the fastest heartbeat of any living thing."

My heartbeat is slow, and his is rapid. Then he said, "You're a tortoise, and I'm a hummingbird."

We are running out of things to talk about. I knew it would happen, I just thought it would be later.

Went to an awards luncheon in Hollywood today. The Creative Director from L.A. flew down on the same plane, though not in coach. Not even for fifty minutes would he experience coach. Coach is for others, those who have not had the necessary brilliance and cunning to become a Creative Director from L.A. Coach is for those who did not cut their teeth working for top creative agencies in Portland, Oregon, and then being begged to stay. *Begged.*

At the Four Seasons where the luncheon was held, he sat across from me eating a huge pile of soba noodles. He forked them into his mouth and talked about the ridiculous nature of award shows, how they're all fixed and run by New York has-beens. His noodles looked like worms on a plate. He shoveled them in, sucking noisily as they whipped past his lips. Famous people, his manner implied, may eat as they like.

While he spoke to the other creative directors about the unfairness of the judging, noodles fell down the front of his shirt, to which he had the foresight to attach what looked like the edge of the tablecloth. I watched, mesmerized. More and more I feel totally detached from everything, and am surprised to hear people speak to me and ask for things.

My radio commercial is up for an award. It won't win, because I care.

I asked Michael late last night if we could forget the wedding and just do city hall, and after some initial surprise, he said OK, fine.

But then I thought about seeing Lana and Yvonne and Ray and Dusty and Beth and everybody and I decided I wanted one anyway. A small one, a casual one. I just want to show up, like a party. So over breakfast this morning I told him I had changed my mind, that we should have the wedding.

Now whenever I bring up the wedding, Michael narrows

his eyes into slits and nods at every suggestion, as though he is biding his time until the attendants arrive with my Thorazine shot.

This morning at dawn as she was stealing our newspaper, the crazy South African landlady stepped in a big yellow runny dog turd on the sidewalk in front of our building. I looked out the bedroom blinds and she was hopping around on one foot dressed in a Christian Dior pantsuit and a sequined hairnet, mad as hell. It was like Halloween and Christmas all rolled into one.

Later, Michael calls my office from Union Square, where he has just purchased a headset for his new StarTac cellular telephone. He tells me how great it is that he can walk down the street with his hands free, talking on the phone with nothing but small undetectable earphones in his ears. I imagine him walking down O'Farrell, talking animatedly with his hands in his pockets.

"People will think you're a paranoid schizophrenic," I say.

"Yes," he says pleasantly.

I go to see Reuben. I tell him how I am struggling with the wedding plans. How it seems too overwhelming and time-consuming to even begin.

He tells me the golf story.

"I decided I was going to learn golf. I was a pretty athletic guy, in those days. I had my own practice in Pebble Beach; there was a golf course within a few miles. I bought a whole set of customized clubs, with special handles, designed for my height and weight. Then I hired a golf pro to tutor me.

"On our first lesson, we go to the driving range and I begin to swing with all my might. I am going to hit that ball as hard as I can, which I know is pretty hard. I miss every ball in the bucket. Finally I get down to the last ball, and I'm mortified. I just want to get it over with, so without even looking I swing, and it connects, and sails three hundred yards, perfectly straight ahead. My golf instructor was so amazed he held the sides of his head and fell to the ground.

"Just a nice easy swing . . . ," Reuben murmurs. Then he says, "I never hit another golf ball."

This seems to me to be another story, but he stops there.

I am the last one to get married, of the tight ring we formed as girls. Yvonne, Lana, and I. We made a bet one night in 1981, sitting downstairs at Larry Blake's in Berkeley drinking kamikazes, that whoever was the last to get married would be owed something. A consolation prize, I see now, although at the time it was viewed as a reward.

Yvonne married first, an overachiever. She was the only one of us to marry before age thirty. Eight years later at age thirty-seven came Lana, the rebel, who married Raul a year after giving birth to Isabel.

I will bring up the rear, a scant ten months past Lana. The dark horse, I win. Though now I don't remember what I win.

I am hurrying down Sacramento Street to my dentist's office and from a distance I see this tall well-built Greek man that

I used to work with when I was a secretary, and that I slept with a few times. He was married to an ice-skater named Dawn. I had just been jilted after a long affair with a devastating Indian man who went back to his old girlfriend who was also from India. The Greek man helped me get over this, in my apartment during lunch. His wife, he said, was away a lot at ice-skating exhibitions. Removing his clothes and folding them carefully on my bedroom chair he admitted to me that, though he loved her, she did not begin to fathom his complexities.

Although I recognize the tall Greek right away I pretend not to see him, and he pretends not to see me. We walk right by each other, close enough to touch.

In a true universe, I would say, "Still cheating on your wife?" And he would reply, "Still fucking married men?"

Instead we pass each other silently. Cowards and charlatans, unite.

Michael went to return a video tonight, around ten. The place on Lyon, near the projects. As he pushed the door open, the store's guard dog came racing toward him. In the last moment, he closed the door again, and stepped back as the dog went crazy inside.

They had just closed, but had forgotten to draw the latch on the door.

When he comes back, he tells me what happened. He is out of breath from hurrying back to tell me.

I hug him tight, especially his head, which is the most important part of him. He buries his head in my neck, and closes his eyes.

I will kill anyone who hurts him.

Someone saw Graham today and was telling me how great he was doing, and I experienced what my friend Jill calls a Grand Klong: a sudden rush of shit to the heart.

"A Grand Klong is when you look in your rearview mirror and you see the police car," Jill says. "And then there's a Petit Klong.

"A Petit Klong is where you're talking about somebody and they arrive, but they have not heard their name."

Nothing had better happen to Jill, is all I have to say. Because now with Graham gone, I'm down to my last crazy person.

Meanwhile, I am going to look for my wedding dress tomorrow. Reuben said I shouldn't go alone, but Lana is in New Mexico and I can't ask Beth, whose marriage is in the implosion process. Yvonne just had a baby, so she never goes anywhere.

Reuben said that when I go to get my dress, I should pay a lot of attention to what comes up.

"This is a time for deep emotions," he said. "Don't try to be a warrior."

I found my wedding dress. At a small boutique in Palo Alto, which specializes in dresses made at the turn of the century. The place where we're getting married is a Victorian mansion in Sausalito. A theme has emerged, seemingly on its own.

The woman at the shop was round and pretty, with long brown hair and brown eyes. Fiona. I instantly wanted to be in her kitchen, drinking tea and exchanging confidences while she pulled cake tins out of her oven.

She tells me her life story. An expert, she has been married several times. Once for five weeks, once for five years, and once for six days.

"It was the six-day one that really got me," she says. She left him after six days because of the prenuptial agreement he had drafted. At the last second before signing it, she lifted up the top sheet and on the underneath carbon copy there was a clause. A clause he had written in, entitling him to her house and property.

"Something made me lift it up." She frowns and looks sharply out the shop window, as if he might be coming up the walk right now, with more falsified documents.

Her current marriage is in its sixth year. "He's my best friend," she says.

I am your new best friend, I don't say.

As we talk I dig for details unself-consciously. I feel I have a right. I want to know why she didn't get an annulment to the six-day marriage. She said it was because they did it in Vegas, so it was a final sale.

She helps me on and off with the dresses, smoothing the slips and straightening hems. In the back of my mind I am aware that she reminds me uncannily of Leigh, the spare mother I lost.

I keep talking myself out of the resemblance.

I try on a lot of dresses which make me look like a miscast chambermaid. A very well-dressed Victorian woman, about to go to bed.

And then I try on the Dress, a knotted-French-linen lace sheath, the color of milky tea. I look in the mirror and I see a woman from 1910, with my face, who coincidentally is also about to be married. I turn around. The Leigh-Fiona woman looks on, but something is wrong. Something is missing.

"I know what you need," she says. I instinctively believe her. If she were to say, Clown shoes, I would say, Yes. Great.

She digs around in a trunk and finds a headpiece of wax and glycerin pearls, from the turn of the century. She arranges it across my brow. I look in the mirror again. Time spins backward. I turn around and face her.

She mouths the word "perfect," rolling her eyes in disgust. I have no right to be so lucky. She understands this, being another woman.

I look back into the mirror. I acknowledge that the person I see, though not me, is beautiful. At the same time I feel worried. I say, "It looks so bridal."

She leans forward and whispers, "You're a bride."

I am. This is the first time I have felt this. Ridiculously, my eyes grow wet.

I buy both the dress and the headpiece, along with a long silk slip from the thirties, which, incredibly, is the same exact shade as the dress and also fits me perfectly. Through the entire process I can't stop thinking of Leigh.

Before I give Fiona my credit card, she has a few tests she needs to run.

She says, "Sit down."

I sit down. It doesn't bind anywhere.

"Now hug me. You're going to be hugging a lot of people that day." I hug her. I close my eyes.

It is Leigh.

I don't let go for a long time. Because I don't know when I am going to see her again.

June

We boil at different degrees.

RALPH WALDO EMERSON

A hot day. We went to Baker Beach and waded. Yellow tugboats chugged under the orange bridge against the blue sky.

Michael, who is from Brooklyn, kept saying, "Oh yeah. This is a terrible city."

We ate salami sandwiches and drank beer.

Afterward he turned to me and said, "You know what's great about the ocean? It makes your fingers taste like pumpkin seeds."

I can't leave him, probably ever.

Today I had my first dress fitting.

Fiona describes how she is going to design a long veil to attach to the headpiece. She will renovate the dress and repair the tiny holes that the years have produced; the holes which I don't see but she sees. Then she is going to hem the vintage slip and take the leftover silk and make bouquet ribbons. There is enough for four bouquets, she announces with mild authority. I am going to have bridesmaids, after all. Lana and Beth and Yvonne. Somewhere in my mind I have known this all along.

As I drive home from her shop, I feel as though I am watching a retrospective of my life. I see my grandmother serving me a bowl of *café con leche* at her house in Pasadena. I see Yvonne and me making perfume out of Comet, and my first pair of red P.F. Flyers. I see the agonized face of my mother when I came home two hours late from first grade. I see Karla McBride and Lynda Yee and Vicki Whitehall. I see my Bluebird uniform and the brown house on Eastman Street, where we moved when I was seven. I see the red plaid bag my father packed the night he left Eastman Street for good. I see my face reflected in the brass Blue Chip stamps table lamp as my mother closed the door behind him. I see David Whalen, standing under a plastic arch of fake roses at the junior-high dance, and Lana, the same night, crying because she had finally kissed Curt Armstrong and he had bad breath. I see Dusty showing me how to perfect the arch of my eyebrows, using an old toothbrush and hairspray. I see Leigh at my high-school graduation, laughing at something Jack has said, her black hair lifting in the wind. I see the crystal heart necklace she gave me that I lost the same night. I see Jackson Kent standing in line at college orientation as I plummet into love with him, my whole skin thrumming as he looks past me at someone else. I see the semiprofessional basketball player and me dancing at a nightclub in 1988; I see him reaching down to slap the ground, in time to Peter Gabriel's "Sledgehammer." I see my mother driving me away from his house, my clothes loaded into the backseat, the car door flying open as we speed away. I see myself skipping down Folsom Street in a long dress and engineer boots after landing my first job as a copywriter. I see the first time I saw Graham, wearing his Prince Valiant haircut and big maroon pants and orange Vans. I see the little blue Fiat I bought from Dusty, with the torn seats. I see myself climbing the cliff, alone, at Red Sand Beach in Maui on my thirty-fourth birthday. I see the thumb of Michael's left hand as he reached across the table at the Rite Spot Bar and Grill to hold my hand for the first time.

I cry throughout. I have no idea where this is coming from.

Reuben says that in many cultures, the wedding ceremony and all of its rituals are much the same as a funeral: a transition into another phase of life.

It is like dying and being reborn, if you believe in an afterlife. If you don't believe in an afterlife, then you're toast.

I was in a meeting at work regarding a new brand of women's cross-trainer shoes when Margaret, this very petite redheaded Irish Catholic, said, "Have sex early if you want a girl."

We all leaned in.

Margaret said that if day 1 is the first day of your period, then you should have sex on days 11 and 12 and that way you will have a girl.

She explained that when the egg comes down on the fourteenth day and you ovulate, all the male sperm from day 11 that aggressively rushed in and got there first will be dead.

"They can't hang," she said.

The females are slow and steady. When the egg comes down, they are the only ones standing.

Damn the women are smarter, is what I was thinking.

Then she pointed her small white finger at us and said, "Do you realize you can only get pregnant for twenty-four hours a month?"

We all feel gypped by the twenty-four-hour window. It seems to decrease our authority. I myself felt I could get pregnant at any time, without even having sex. Like an amoeba, subdividing. I could just decide.

"Those fucking nuns lied," says Margaret.

In the dream Graham is back and I've gone to see him at his new apartment. When I go to leave, my car has been stolen, and then I find it but the seats are backward.

I know Reuben will love the backward seats part at our session today, and he does.

"You need to pay attention to the back draft," he proclaims. "What has come before."

I sit with this. It feels uncomfortable.

"What else do you think the backward seats mean?" he asks.

I feel I know this one. I say, "Well, it's true you should look behind you. But you can't drive that way."

Reuben nods.

"That's something else the dream is trying to tell you—

the car represents your persona. Persona was the mask that the Greek actors wore. The car symbolizes this facade."

Then he adds, "Especially in California.

"The car is not the deepest part of the trip, but it is the vehicle," he says. "As Graham was a vehicle for you."

He says this and then he smiles a little. Tying the bow.

I think about how Reuben has a Reuben persona. Friendly and interested like a long-nosed dog. An old dog. An old wise dog that has seen everything and can talk to birds.

Toward the end of our session I tell him about how I'm using my dreams in my work and how it's all cross-pollinating in this alchemistic fashion. I tell him how, in my writing, I've discovered a second voice. As I say this Reuben hauls himself out of his customary slouch and looks very alive and interested, as if he has just discovered he has bingo.

"Carl Jung had a second voice which he called Persona Number Two," he says.

How Germanic, I thought. Give them numbers.

"Jung seemed to think that, eventually, the stronger voice would emerge."

"I don't want the stronger voice to emerge," I say. "I want both." I am conscious of ordering it up. I'll have the cake with ice cream, please.

When I leave, Reuben follows me out. We've gone into overtime, which we've never done. I didn't even know you could.

As I descend the stairs, he says, "I think we're going to see some fascinating things in the next few weeks."

I felt he was waving a wand over my head when he said this, but he was behind me so I couldn't know for certain.

. . .

Last night I dreamed the police impounded my car. My first thought as I wake up is that Reuben isn't helping.

Then I lie in bed and feel smug about the fact that my car is safe in the garage.

Tonight Michael and I ate dinner in the kitchen with the radio on. There seemed to be nothing to say about anything. I felt surprised.

In the end it all comes down to two faces staring at each other across a table. They should *tell* people that.

Later I was lying flat on my back with my Powerbook on my chest, typing in bed. My head was crooked up on a pillow at a right angle.

"You're doing terrible things to your spine," Michael said.

A few seconds went by, and then he said, "That was my mother speaking through me."

I'm severely PMS. What my friend Jill calls, Pardon Me, Sybil.

Michael wants me to go back on the Pill, which I went off after reading the tiny information pamphlet. He doesn't like me to have PMS. "You were an angel while you were on the Pill," he says.

When he talks about my being an angel, with a supercilious look of dissatisfaction on his face, I want to harm him.

Then get yourself an angel, I want to say. Let me help you meet the angels.

If he gets a hangnail, we all have to race for an ambulance. But I can't have anything go wrong with me. This seems to be the deal.

I realize anew that it's not the purchase price of love, it's the *maintenance*. That's where they screw you.

A year is far too long a time to be engaged. Much, much too long.

We had been bickering all day, a Sunday. Michael was on the back porch, smoking an enormous cigar in the dark. He said he thought relationships are just something that keep you from doing what you really want.

That's when I said it. "Well, then maybe you shouldn't get married."

He didn't reply, just glared at me as he fondled his cigar. The kind of man who keeps a jarful of soldiers' ears in his bunker.

Last night I slept far over on my side of the bed, dangling off the edge, one arm touching the floor. He tried to make up once, but I shrugged him off.

This morning I was downtown and by chance I saw Michael walking across the street. I called his name. He turned around, and his face was dead. He wasn't happy to see me.

When I was four, I was swinging from a tree limb, and suddenly I lost my grip. I fell to the ground, and the wind was knocked out of me. This is what that felt like.

I hurried back to my office and called Lana. Her line was busy. A minute later, the phone rang and it was she. We always go through the exact same things at the exact same time.

Lana is thinking about leaving Raul. And Michael apparently wishes I were in Zambia.

What I said to Lana was, "There's only one thing I know that's worse than this, and that's being alone." She agreed. We are not liberated people.

We talked about how maybe someday Lana and Yvonne and I will live in a big house. A two-story white house, near the ocean. With a fence.

We can decide later if it is to be electric or not.

I was driving south across the Golden Gate Bridge, and a car had stopped at the northbound toll plaza, in the free direction. A disembodied voice boomed from the loud-speakers above: *"THERE IS NO STOPPING OR TURN-ING AROUND. YOU ARE COMMITTED TO THE BRIDGE."*

A morning of the most bizarre and desperate meetings imaginable at the agency, all about the new Strategy, which the account people always say is coming but never does.

I feel haggard, as though I have been living the same day over and over again. It occurs to me that I detest advertising and that this fact isn't going to go away, that actually as I approach forty it will intensify. I begin to understand that I am not going to be allowed a second, more honorable lifetime, where I teach handicapped children and write politically correct musicals and know Toni Morrison.

Then I flog myself over the fact that I should be happy. I am making six figures and working on the largest account in the country in the most beautiful city in the world. And every few months someone calls from New York to try to get me to interview. I am at my peak.

I am at my peak and from here you can really see the crucifixions.

I have a dream where Graham is dressed in a giant clown suit. He takes off the orange-wigged headpiece to show me that it is just him. He is smiling in the dream, and everything is fine.

I told Reuben about it. He said, "In the Zuni culture there is a ceremonial dance where everyone dances in one direction, and a clown runs in the other direction, poking fun at the rest of the dancers.

"It would be helpful if you thought of Graham as the clown."

Suddenly I am teeming with clowns.

Before I leave, I ask Reuben, "Shouldn't I be getting over this by now?"

I am crying, but I pretend not to be.

"It's only been three months," he said. "You'd grieve longer over a dog."

"Oh," I said. Nobody ever told me.

Last night we ate pasta at Rose Pistola. Before long we were talking about Madonna. Michael thinks that she is a ridiculous slut. He is too clever to say this directly, but he gets the message across. He knows I like her, that I listen to her tapes in the gym. He's seen the photograph from the Halloween when Lana and Yvonne and I went as Material Girls, the three of us wearing crosses and fake moles.

Michael said she was a publicity-mad media-invented dehumanized parody of a human being. I said, "Look at Howard Stern. Look at Marilyn Manson.

"Dennis Rodman," I said, grasping at straws.

"If she were a man, no one would lift an eyebrow," I said.

He agrees but looks upset. Every time we talk about Madonna, we end up like this. You would be surprised how often Madonna comes up.

Finally I said, "Look, this dinner is costing about eighty dollars, and I don't want to talk about Madonna."

That seemed to make sense to him. We had spumoni, came home, and made love. Afterward he brought me some orange juice, and we laughed about how when you hold down the Cow's ears he looks like Karl Lagerfeld.

The copywriter down the hall is engaged, I just heard. When I saw him today in the lobby, I asked him when he was getting married.

"September twenty-first," he said.

"How do you like being engaged?" I asked.

He leaned against the wall and said that it's funny I should ask, because last night over dinner he had discussed postponing the wedding.

I wonder if it was before or after he had eaten. This is only about the third time I have spoken to him, so I can't ask.

"I just don't know if we're compatible," he said. He was now leaning at a more pronounced angle, as if he might fall down. "I just think it might be better to postpone."

Postpone, I thought. A euphemism. *Body* instead of *corpse*. *Funeral director* versus *mortician*. I wish I could laugh. I would like to throw my head back and laugh, for about an hour.

"I'm not head over heels in love," he said. His eyes looked haunted. "Maybe I'm not supposed to be. Maybe this is mature love."

I say nothing. Advice, I know, would be pointless. I am talking to someone with an arrow through his head.

"But maybe I'm just not the kind of person that's supposed to get married. I mean last night she asked me, 'Are you a fighter, or are you a quitter?'"

We both look at each other, as though we are waiting for something to happen.

"I'm a quitter," he said. "I've always been a quitter."

When he slumped back into his office, he looked exactly like a man who is about to pull a .38 out of his desk drawer and shoot himself. But that would be too neat. It's much more interesting than that, I understand.

Last night on the phone Ilene told me she doesn't want us to throw rice. She said it makes birds explode, which in turn spreads disease. She said she would turn right around and go back to New York if we did it. She said, "That's all I ask."

"That's it? That's all you ask?" I said. I was hoping to get some sort of verbal agreement.

"For now," she said.

I have created this, is what I thought. This is what my toadying has brought about. All the little cards and letters and Harry and David I felt it necessary to send her.

Reuben said he once had a woman patient whose mother-in-law was coming to stay with her and her husband for the first time. The mother-in-law was an intimidating woman. Despite everything Reuben tried, the woman remained terrified that the house wouldn't be clean enough, that something would go wrong, and she would be unfavorably judged. When the mother-in-law arrived, the taxi pulled up and deposited her and her ten pieces of Louis Vuitton luggage on their doorstep. As she stepped onto the porch, the family's golden retriever, who had just spent the morning rolling in fresh dog shit, bounded forward and jumped all over the mother-in-law.

Reuben listened to her distraught story and then said to the woman, "With a dog like that, what do you need me for?"

As usual he insists I pay attention to my feelings regarding Ilene and all of this. He claims I don't even have to do anything, but just know what's going on.

"What *is* going on?" I ask.

What's nice about therapy is that I may ask direct questions. I needn't act as if I know what I'm doing.

"You're getting married," he says. "You're starting a new life, independent of your family."

I've upped my sessions to twice a week, with Reuben. I feel no shame about using every available crutch.

I can't believe I used to do all this alone.

I consider how there are numerous people willing to explain diamonds to you, but no one explains this. For this you have to hire a bearded man and pay him $150 an hour.

July

It is better to marry than to burn.

1 CORINTHIANS

I was flying to a commercial shoot in New York with Clark and a producer named Micky Love. The plane was cruising at thirty thousand feet when the pilot came on the loudspeaker.

"Some of you may have noticed some fluid leaking out of the right wing of the plane. . . . Don't worry, this is not jet fuel . . . it's hydraulic fluid."

I do not feel the relief that this announcement suggests I ought.

"We've pressurized the leak, and we have two other compartments of hydraulic fluid."

A few minutes go by. Many people are spending a lot of time looking out at the right wing, which is steadily dripping a clear fluid. The rest of us on the other side of the plane are watching the people who are watching the wing.

The pilot comes back on, "Oh, well, hey listen—there are some storms in New York, so instead of landing at JFK, we're going to land in Chicago. . . ."

Since our lifeblood is running out, is the rest of his sentence. We finish it for him in our minds. I look at Clark, smile with what I hope looks like wry humor, and reach into my bag. This seems an excellent time for the sixteenth Valium. I dry swallow. Clark orders a double Stoli, refusing to pay. He'll pay when we bloody land, he says.

Then I call Michael on the air phone, but he's not in his office. I leave a message saying only that we are landing in Chicago instead of New York. I don't want him to worry. Actually what I want is to cry senselessly into the phone, which I plan to do later, if I am still alive and there is a larger part of me than my teeth left.

An hour later, as we are about to land at O'Hare, a deep moaning sound comes out of the wings of the plane. We slam down onto the runway. No comment from the cockpit. Nothing from the Don't Worry men.

The stewardesses beam as we leave the plane. For some reason they are all in terrific moods. I am aware that I have been lied to, but consider myself lucky not to be pinwheeling across a cornfield in flames.

By the time I finally talk to Michael I am in New York and feel that I have probably made the whole thing up.

Manhattan. The Royalton Hotel. A lavish lobby, ghost furniture draped in white muslin, serpentine-shaped banisters. Long slim impossibly dark hallways with portholes leading nowhere, into more blackness.

I am led upstairs by a young man who is dressed like a

bellboy from the forties. He is the perfect bellboy, making small talk with flawless light charm. He actually has rosy cheeks. He seems artificial. I have the feeling that around midnight I will wake up like the doomed astronauts in the *Martian Chronicles*, a claw on my shoulder as I try to plunge out the window toward safety.

We arrive at a small gray concrete room. There is a bed and a chair. Shower, no bath. Two hundred and eighty-five dollars.

I never take the first room.

The next room, as always, is slightly better. It has an extra chair, flanking a small round table in what would be a living area, were there any area.

The mini-bar. When the bellman leaves, I make my selection.

A small mixed-candy bag with one miniature Tootsie Roll, one miniature Necco (twelve wafers), two mini–Reese's peanut-butter cups, one mini-Snickers, one Fire Ball, one Hershey's Kiss, one orange LifeSaver, one Lemon Head, one Smarties, one barrel-shaped root-beer hard candy, and one horrible oblong sesame log thing. All in a tiny cellophane sack, tied with a black ribbon with "Jonathan Morr" written on it, inexplicably.

Eighteen dollars.

New York is pure cyanide. The idea of New York, however, is marvelous.

It was the eighteenth hour of the New York shoot, sometime after 2 a.m., and we were all on the set, talking about sleep.

I explained how I need my feet to be outside of the covers at all times.

Bill, the account supervisor, says, "I need to be as tightly tucked in as possible. Cold air on the feet is death."

"I need them to be free," I say. Meaning my feet.

My new partner Clark says he sleeps with his feet outside the covers too. I feel this is significant. Everyone is looking at us.

"You sleep with your feet hanging out?" repeats the client, and shivers.

Then the client, whose ski club once poured Miracle-Gro in his mouth when he fell asleep with his mouth open, announces, "I need to be fully tucked in." He says it as though it is the agency's responsibility.

I describe how at a hotel I have to go all the way around the bed and untuck the whole thing. Not just my side.

"I can go with the free-range covers but not the dangling," says Bill.

"Whether I'm tired or not I can fall asleep in five to thirty seconds," says Clark. I consider the possibility of this.

"You are such a liar," I say. He and I burst out laughing.

"You go music or buzzer?" Bill asks Chad, the research guy whom I once referred to as That Handsome Young Guy in Research, which I am sure they told him because ever since then I've felt uncomfortable.

"Buzzer," says Chad.

"Right on," says Bill. "I used to go music, but now the music just incorporates right into my dream. I've got to have the buzzer or I'm done."

Clark says, "I like to be fully naked, with my watch on."

"What's up with that?" asks Bill.

"Earthquake," says Clark.

"I buy everything about that except the watch thing," says Bill. "What, you need to know what time the earthquake starts?"

"King or queen?" asks Clark, ignoring this.

"I don't like the king," says Bill.

"How so?"

"Too big. Too much room. I like to be in control of the whole situation. I like to know the borders."

He goes on, "I think I only have enough body temperature to heat up a queen. I like to heat up the whole bed for when I start to move."

"A thrasher," I say.

"Oh yeah. I'm a thrasher," says Bill.

"I can't do flannel," says Chad from Research, suddenly.

"I hate flannel," I say.

"I'm flannel all year long," says Bill. He seems proud. "I like to block out the world with my pillows," he says.

"How many?" I ask.

"Two separate down pillows," he explains. "One big fluffy one that I sink my head into, and one smaller one that I smash into my face so I get that underground subterranean feeling."

"Window open or shut?" I ask.

"Open. All year," says Bill. "Colder the better."

"I need to feel the air on my face," says Chad. He seems almost unbearably handsome as he says this. This may be the moment in time when he peaks, like a bosc pear.

He turns to Bill and states, "But you like sleeping in a king-size bed when you're by yourself."

He knows this for some reason. Maybe it's because he's from Research.

"Oh yeah," says Bill.

"Do you have a side?" I ask Bill.

"Absolutely. You?"

"Definitely. Always," I say.

"Left or right?" he asks.

"Left," I say.

"Left facing the bed or left to you?"

"My left," I say.

"Me too," says Bill. "That's my side too."

"But the alarm's on the other side, right?" says Chad.

"That's right," I say. "The alarm's usually on the other side. And I have the telephone."

He nods knowingly.

There is something going on here, but to name it would be to change it. I can't sleep with strange men anymore, so I soak all of this in. The information.

While I was in New York, Michael actually called the catering company, and they faxed back a menu suggestion. He presented this to me today, over a small picnic at Muir Beach.

It is right except for one thing: the sesame chicken with Asian dipping sauce. I want chicken satay skewers with peanut sauce.

"Done," Michael says.

We will also be having endive spears with Gorgonzola vinaigrette. Polenta cups with walnut filling. Then comes the mandatory poached salmon and thinly sliced beef.

I feel a sudden glee. Somehow I saw myself with large

aluminum-foil trays of lasagna, jugs of Gallo Hearty Burgundy. A checked oilcloth flapping in the wind, and maybe someone standing with a shotgun pointed at Michael. The fact that I am going to have polenta cups with walnut filling is spectacular.

I described our menu to a few close friends and colleagues today. Maybe ten or twelve.

What I find about wedding plans is everyone wants to talk about them when I don't, and then as soon as I do feel like talking about my wedding plans, their eyes glaze over and I can see them wishing they were dead.

Tonight after work, Michael came upstairs with the mail.

In it was a postcard from Graham, who is in the Southwest now.

"Did you read it?" I asked Michael. He had taken an unusually long time coming up the front steps.

"Of course," he said. Then he added, "If there was anything in it that would have hurt you, you never would have gotten it."

There are people who would object to this. They are people who were probably protected throughout their childhood by a loving father, and who have outgrown the need for one.

I save Graham's postcard for later. I just gaze at the impossibly square handwriting and put it in my desk drawer. I hoard it, along with other sketches and caricatures he has drawn.

Graham is on a great adventure. But so am I.

. . .

We have just culled the guest list. It fluctuates between eighty-eight and ninety-six, our target number being ninety. Some ruthless editing took place.

It's not people who won't be attending our wedding. It's people who won't be our friends anymore. To deny this would be pointless.

I imagine long, elaborate rationalizations about why we omitted each of the people we crossed out. I see them confronting me; in my mind it is always at a supermarket, under the glare of fluorescent lights. I need a pat answer, something I can memorize.

It was just family.

We had to keep it small.

I don't like you. It took me until this moment to fully realize that.

I feel there should also be an honorable mention list, of people we wanted to invite but couldn't because they were inexorably connected to people we didn't want to invite but would have had to invite if we had invited them.

We are having dinner at Powell's Soul Kitchen, discussing whether I will take Michael's last name and drop my own.

"I wouldn't ask you to . . . ," he says, but looks pleased. That's OK because I'm not going to, I think to myself.

We stare at each other for a while, raising our eyebrows every so often. I notice, not for the first time, that he is handsome. No one else looks like him. He would be impossible to replace.

We drive to the Theater Artaud to hear the Kronos Quartet perform. Each piece takes me to a different place in my mind. I forget that I am listening to music, which seems to be the best kind of music.

Afterward, we talk about whether we will have a girl or a boy, someday. It is a running debate, as if we are ordering a new car. I mention the name Raphael for a boy. I think he will laugh.

"It's a beautiful name," Michael says.

At home in the kitchen, we dance to Chet Baker singing "My Funny Valentine." We dance the whole song, and then we dance past that.

Addressed invitations for four hours after work. Now I feel like a baked potato that has its insides scooped out and mashed and then stuffed back in its skin.

After I've driven to the post office and dropped them off, I call my mother. She takes this opportunity to express regret that her name and Don's weren't on the invitation. She doesn't understand why it's just my name and Michael's at the top.

I tell her because it implies a transaction, the bride being passed from the parents to the husband. I tell her I'm thirty-six years old and not anybody's child anymore, and that since I'm paying for the wedding along with Michael, it's really our wedding. We planned it and it's ours.

"You didn't put my name on the invitation when you married Don," I said. This doesn't make sense, but it does.

I think I have her, when she murmurs, "I hope you have a daughter."

. . .

Today Michael left for his annual Death Valley motorcycle trip. He and several other middle-aged men will be wheeling into hundred-degree heat, pretending to be Peter Fonda in 1969. Harmless, unless he spins off the road and becomes pizza.

Meanwhile at work, Clark and I presented the casting choices for the new cross-trainer TV spot. Another client meeting where they voice every possible objection and criticism and then say, "I'm comfortable."

Then they stare at us until we get the idea just how much money five hundred thousand dollars is. Until we feel it in our bones.

Around four o'clock, Michael came back from his Death Valley Peter Fonda Impersonation Festival. He looked worn and empty. I made him his favorite dinner: unfried chicken from the Oprah book and red potato salad from the Susan Powter book.

After dinner, he kept talking about how much water he drank, over a gallon a day. He worried that he had sweated out all his essential vitamins and minerals. Later I brought him some vitamins and aspirin and turned out the light. He had fallen asleep with his reading glasses on, a copy of the *New Yorker* in his hands. The Jewish Man exhibit.

A trip downtown to buy Michael's wedding band. It is white gold, with scrolled yellow-gold edging. They sized it for him in the store.

When I paid for it, Michael said, "Congratulations. You've just purchased your first husband. With the proper care and maintenance, he should last a good ten years."

The saleslady laughed, after she made sure that I laughed.

I was thinking, No, most marriages break up right around the seven-year mark.

I was also thinking how great it was that his ring cost me eight hundred dollars and my ring cost him seven thousand.

He admired a Raymond Weil watch while we were there. Tomorrow I will go back and buy it for him.

I'll still be way ahead.

In two days I leave for Paris, to shoot the five-hundred-thousand-dollar athletic-shoe commercial with the French director, who looks exactly like Uncle Fester from *The Addams Family*. He is bald and wears a black turtleneck and black pants and black shoes and black socks. I wouldn't be amazed if he stuck a lightbulb in his mouth and it worked.

I feel ambivalent about Paris, because Michael won't be there, and Graham won't be there. Then I castigate myself for not being happy. It is Paris, after all.

More and more I resent all activity. I don't want to do anything except nap and finesse the honeymoon and read Margaret Atwood and Fay Weldon, who obviously don't believe in marriage at all.

In other news, they separated those Siamese twin girls today. They were joined at the stomach.

"Just like us," Michael said.

. . .

Flew to Paris yesterday to do the commercial. I did OK on the flight until about the seventh hour, when I became lonely and disheveled and began obsessing on what Michael was doing now that I was hurtling toward another continent. I doubted that my powers of psychic surveillance crossed the Atlantic.

I tried to call him, but the air phones didn't work over Iceland. After I had landed, it was too late to call him.

The hotel is stunning, much nicer than we'll be able to afford for our honeymoon. It's too fine to enjoy alone; it goads me. I don't want to be here right now, would like to press a button and be instantly back home. Just a nice little red button on the side of the hotel bed marked RETURN, like on my computer. When is *that* coming?

Nothing superior has been invented in my lifetime. It is all chemotherapy and cellular phones.

Four hours after we arrived, the shoot was canceled. The French authorities had misunderstood the date on the location permits.

Unfortunately, they explained to our producer Micky as he suffered an apoplexy, the site was unavailable for the next two days in question, due to a large wedding that was taking place for a local fragrance giant.

They really do have a marvelous sense of humor. It's going to cost the client about ninety thousand dollars.

I'll stay the weekend and fly back Sunday. I am bathed with relief.

This proves two things: (1) As a professional, I am a failure, and (2) I am controlling the world with my mind.

I went to look at the Hôtel Panthéon, where we are staying for our honeymoon. The room was very sweet, with a canopy bed and a small reading chaise. They let me take photographs to show Michael, even though the room was occupied by another couple who were out sight-seeing. When I develop these pictures, I will be able to piece together their lives from the belongings and the disarray. I will know whether they are in love, whether they will last.

They are us, is what I imagine.

Wandered through the Rue du Buci, the daily open-air market. I purchased three pairs of shoes. In this country it seems possible to buy no pairs of shoes, or three pairs, but never just one or two. Also a bag of cherries and mini-bananas. Michael would have loved the minute white radishes, the array of roasted chickens, the soft cheeses. The huge pans of scrambled eggs with truffles, and paella.

I photographed the fruit for him. The tiny ladybug tomatoes.

I don't want to miss him so much. I want to be able to turn it down. Instead I live with a rock in my heart. I walk through Paris, carrying it. Maybe this is what they mean by the ball and chain.

.   .   .

The eve of my return. I have just spent four days eating cheese. Cheese for breakfast, cheese and salad for lunch, and after dinner, I choose from a selection of cheeses.

It strikes me that my arms are as big as bolognas; swollen, outsized. I walk for hours around Paris, corpulent and alone. I drag my feet like an angry six-year-old.

My wedding dress has short sleeves.

Called Michael and wept into the phone.

He said, "Everything's all right."

"Do you still love me?" I asked.

"Of course."

He hasn't seen me, is why. He doesn't know.

I am on the plane flying next to a French teenage girl. Her arms are like sticks. The stewardess brings me a bowl of macadamia nuts and cashews. I feel she is hostile as she pushes banana liqueurs and Godiva chocolates on me after the dinner service. Her arms are normal.

I can't stop looking at people's arms.

An overwhelming sense of panic and fear. I have to lose twenty pounds before the wedding. I have to get on the ground and out of this airplane. And I have to go back in time.

What I'm realizing is, I am too old to get married. I am an old maid, with fat arms.

I can't possibly get away with this.

Michael picked me up at customs. He hugged me very tightly and then he discovered his watchband had broken,

and his chronograph watch had popped off at the airport.
Then he spent an hour obsessing about it.

I believe this means his time is up.

Dreamed about my old high-school boyfriend last night. I
am telling him I am getting married, and he has no reaction.
He is not happy for me, but he is happy to see me. He leads
me away to a bedroom, where I say, "Wait, I can't do this."

"Even in your dreams, you're faithful," says Reuben.
Making a note of it.

In the past week I have dreamed of Jackson Kent, also.
Jackson and I met in a poetry class, taught by Philip Levine,
who looked like a bricklayer and who recently won the
Pulitzer. Jackson resembled a young Brando. I thought.

I feel I'm in the wrong tunnel. I want to go forward, but I
keep taking the wrong exit and going back. I am plagued by
advance nostalgia for my single days.

I was watching the movie *Truly Madly Deeply*, where the
heroine's boyfriend comes back from the dead and at first
she's elated but then she just wants him out. She wants the
bathroom back again.

Of course the first thing she does once he does dematerialize is buy a toothbrush and bring it over to this other guy's
house. And you can see where they're going to end up
married.

What Anaïs Nin says is that the dream is always running
ahead. To catch up, to live for the moment in unison with it,
that is the miracle.

. . .

People were supposed to return the response cards, but many of them haven't. These are people I naturally assumed would be thrilled and would reply immediately. Now I have to call them and ask them about it, and I have to be nice and not say what I would like to say.

"Hello? I'm sorry to bother you but is it too much *fucking trouble* to send that little card back? I put a stamp on it. But maybe you need me to come over to your house and carry you to the mailbox."

In light of these developments there ought to be a way to uninvite the people who are disturbing me. I need a longshoreman named Vito to visit these people and quietly but clearly uninvite them. Maybe rough them up a little.

I want others to experience pain. I believe it would lessen mine.

I was in Nordstrom buying a strapless bra for my wedding dress, when a woman approached me and held out a black Donna Karan nightshirt. She was around seventy, with brown-dyed hair wrapped in a chiffon scarf, wearing big orange glasses and sensible shoes. She spoke with a Russian accent.

"Vood you look at this?" she asked, holding out the garment.

There is a loose thread on the hem of the nightshirt. I look back at her eyes, big as apricots behind her glasses.

"First, I vant you to look at the name on the label." She points carefully with one finger. She is giving me the answers to a test that will be coming up later, her manner suggests.

I look. It says Donna Karan Intimates.

"A pathetic voomin. Now look at za price." She points again.

I do. Eighty-eight dollars.

I look back at her. For the first time in weeks, I am fully present.

Then she takes this loose black thread on the hem and she pulls it. I think she is just making a point, but she keeps pulling it until her arm is fully outstretched.

"Have you ever met her?" she asks. I realize she is talking about Donna Karan.

"No," I say.

"A piece of trash," she says.

For emphasis, she says it like two sentences. A piece. Of trash.

She walks away still holding the nightshirt. I see her headed for the young blond clerk with the pageboy haircut. I am mesmerized, but I look away, because I am also afraid of her. Of what she knows.

I picked up my wedding band yesterday at Shreve's. It has tiny diamonds along the outside that go halfway around the band. I couldn't afford the one with the diamonds that go all the way around. It would cut into my Mexican divorce fund.

While I was there, I discussed engraving with Reed, our salesman. Reed told me about an engaged couple who had FOREVER engraved along the inside of their bands. They wanted the word FOREVER repeated as many times as it would fit, all along the inside of the rings. He had it done, and delivered the rings. They called him back three days later and asked if he could take the rings back, return their money, and sand the engraving off. He said, "I guess so."

. . .

This morning Michael said that I was a gift from God to him. He said he thought it was because he had started volunteering for Project Open Hand, shelling peas for four hours every Tuesday. I give money to the La Casa de las Madres women's shelter and to San Francisco Suicide Prevention, but not that much.

I don't know how I got Michael. Maybe I just had a store credit from some other very lonely and shitty life.

August

You go not, till I set you up a glass
Where you may see the inmost part of you.

WILLIAM SHAKESPEARE, *HAMLET*

I called Dusty. I hadn't heard from him in a few months, nor had he responded to my wedding invitation, not even to ridicule it.

I dial his number: 555-7029. He answers on the tenth ring.

"Hey."

"Hey," he said.

"What are you doing?" I asked.

There is a long pause, uncharacteristic of him. He would usually have said, Just sitting here on my ass. Or, Making coleslaw. He does not say either of those things. He lets a little silence well up between us, and then he says, "I've been sick. Actually, I just had my spleen removed."

"Why?" I ask. Doom is creeping up my backbone. Dusty is gay, middle-aged.

"Well, I might as well drop the bomb. Are you sitting down?"

"Yes." Why do people always ask if you're sitting down? I think.

"OK." Big irritated sigh. "I've been HIV positive since 1989."

"Oh." The horrible urge to laugh comes over me, as it always does with shock. On the other end of the line I hear Mary Beth, the Christian QVC host, demonstrating folding silk tote bags from Indonesia.

"I'm so sorry you have to go through this," I say. I am speaking from somewhere above myself. "I love you," I say. I think it is the first time I have ever said it. Then I ask, "Do you need anything?"

Like a new spleen? I think. I am an idiot. Why God doesn't want me to rush home.

"Have you told Ray?" I ask.

Ray is Dusty's best friend.

"I can't," he said, with the dead-set finality of a Texan. I cain't.

When I climbed in bed last night, Michael was already asleep. He smelled like hazelnuts.

I don't tell him about Dusty. Telling him would legitimize something I am not willing to legitimize.

Besides, Dusty's doctors have told him he's going to be around for a long time.

But they lie.

.   .   .

Dusty is the only person I know who still uses butter. He fries chicken in a deep cast-iron skillet. I stopped by one day and found him alone, making a double batch of peach tarts, with fresh peaches. He had rolled the dough from scratch and was piling the tarts, warm, onto tiered servers. We both ate four.

Before he moved to Manhattan from San Francisco in 1990, he once carried a black iron candelabra to my door, unannounced, then walked briskly in, attached it with picture-frame wire, and wrapped a red paisley scarf around the base. And left, screaming away in his orange truck with the gold wheel spokes.

He always wears a white baseball cap, the dirtier the better. He has worn his hair Marine short since before it was the fashion. He rarely shaves but has never had a beard or mustache. He has a permanent stubble, flecked with gray.

He is the worst gossip I have ever known, but has never to my knowledge hurt anyone, man or woman or animal.

He says "fuck" more than anyone I know, somehow making it sound funny each time. In his mouth the word "cool" becomes two syllables. Coo-ull.

Unsatisfied with the words available to most people, he frequently makes up his own words, many of which can be used as a verb or an adjective or a standard of measure. Whump, glunk, gronk.

"You just fuckin' glunk a whole bunch of it on there, and then bake it."

As a chef his measurements are quixotic, known only to him and performed by eye. A recipe has to be done in his presence to be effectively transferred. I have his recipes for roasted mustard turnips, cabbage and rice soup, and corn fritters made with Jiffy mix.

I realize as I write this that I am cataloging. I am storing up what is his.

I call Dusty again.

He sounds bad. We talk about nothing. Nothing is all you get to talk about once the reaper has you in his sights.

Right before we hung up, he told me a story. He told me that as a young man, he had always said he didn't want to live past fifty. He had sworn not to get old, and had specified the age.

"Fifty and that's it," Dusty said. "I used to say that."

He laughed ruefully, as though he had bet on a wrong horse.

Dusty is forty-nine and a half.

Ray phoned this afternoon. I was in bed with a head cold.

"Hedo?"

"Dusty's taken a turn for the worse," he said. "It's Ray," he added, as an afterthought.

"Where are you?" I said.

"I'm at his place." He sounded elaborately casual, as though it hadn't required an airplane. Despite everything, I feel glad that they are together, that Dusty has told him.

"Don't worry about coming out here right away," Ray said. "It's not like he's going to die or anything,"

"OK," I said.

I hung up and dialed United.

"Where are you going?" Michael asked.

"Dusty's dying," I said.

As I pulled up in the cab I sensed something up there, crouched over his apartment building. Waiting.

Walking down the driveway, gravel crunched beneath my rubber sandals. This is one of the sounds of summer, I thought. One of the sounds he will never hear again. I began to cry.

Later, I thought. Not now. Now you smile. You act like this is not happening.

He lay in bed propped on pillows, wrapped in an Indian blanket, surrounded by his friends and his art, which was crammed into every available nook. Tall brightly painted carved figures, embracing in pairs, some of them carrying their own head. Some with their hands clamped over their mouths.

Everyone he knew was either there or on their way. Or they didn't know.

In less than three months he'd lost half his body weight. His hair was mostly gone, smattering his head in spiky gray patches. His head was wrong, lopsided. He looked like the Scarecrow in *The Wizard of Oz* after the flying monkeys had gotten to him. Slumped over, shocked.

And we rush around trying to fit the stuffing back in.

He kept attempting to sit up. He'd succeed for a minute or two and then he'd lie back down.

I held his hand. His hands had shrunk to baby hands, puckered at the wrist. His liver had failed; he had no spleen. The virus had him.

I would have prayed, if I'd felt there was something up there other than that fucking chariot.

But instead I prayed for the chariot.

Dusty had insisted on coming home from the hospital, I find out. So Ray arranged for hospice, which we are all part of, for the time that we are in town. It's a clipboard. A sign-up sheet, like for a school ski trip. *Hospice.* It sounds like such a nice word. It sounds like it has nothing to do with death.

He is on an experimental drug to flush toxins out of his liver, plus prescription marijuana, and painkillers. Even awake he looks asleep. Every so often he'll laugh, a weary chuckle slower than it should be. Each laugh seems a triumph against something.

When he falls into a shallow sleep, we silently file out onto his small roof garden.

Ray squints into the sun, smoking a Camel. His hair, I notice, is now all the color of steel. I realize it has been years since I've seen him.

"When did you start smoking?" I ask.

"This weekend," he says.

I wonder if he is lying, if he has been sneaking smokes all his life. He looks to me now as though he has always smoked, has always had gray hair.

We water Dusty's tomatoes in terra-cotta pots. The plants are bending with fruit. As we pick the overripe ones, the ones that can't wait any longer, Ray looks out at the trees in Gramercy Park, as though I am not there.

"He could live another year," he says. This is not true. We both nod slowly.

This afternoon Ray, ex–star quarterback for the Oakland High class of '76, is in charge of changing Dusty's diapers. Six foot three inches, two hundred and twenty pounds, he crashed around the tiny cluttered apartment, speaking in a loud, boisterous voice about what an asshole Dusty is for having so many cookies in his cupboard. Naming them out loud, like poetry.

"Pinwheels. Mallomars. Chips Ahoy. Flaky Flix."

Yvonne and Lana both call and talk to Dusty for a minute, and then to Ray and me, asking questions.

Ray is wearing Bermuda shorts, a Dallas Cowboys tee shirt, and paper-thin red zori sandals. He spends the day bringing Dusty his mug of Diet Dr Pepper, the only thing he ever drinks. Holding a Merit cigarette to Dusty's lips. Giving him his medicine. Helping him shuffle to the bathroom.

It is probably the most beautiful thing I have ever seen.

After about five hours, I leave and go back to my hotel. I make it a point not to say good-bye.

Ray found Dusty at one point trying to take a shower. He had somehow managed to remove all his clothes. His naked body stood next to the hot-water spigot, which had been turned off when he was in the hospital.

So Ray called the water company, which turned it on, and then Ray gave him a shower.

I think about the loved ones bathing their dead along the banks of the Ganges. I think of, not so long ago, his newborn body washed clean of its birth sac.

. . .

Last night I went again, for the last time.

I made him laugh, once. It felt like lifting a car over my head. A miracle.

At dawn, Ray flew back to Texas, to his wife and two young sons.

After he left, Dusty refused to take any more drugs.

We are on our way to see Michael's daughter, Phoebe, in Vermont. I am meeting Michael there, flying in from New York.

Michael said I could cancel and meet Phoebe some other time, but I feel committed. Although it doesn't seem real, this trip. I feel as though I am standing in for someone, a regular type fiancée without a care in the world. Someone younger and more vibrant, whose friends aren't in liver failure.

Met Phoebe last night and went to dinner.

Michael and I stood in the silk wallpapered foyer of Grace's home. The ceilings were twenty feet high. The drapes were a deep, warm gold; they pulled everything together, I could see that. Grace hands Michael Phoebe's backpack.

"I love your house," I say.

She says nothing. Attractive, she smiles. Of course she's attractive.

"It's really nice to finally meet you," I say.

She does not say, It's nice to meet you, too.

"So," she says. A two-letter sentence. Skillful.

I decide not to make small talk after all. People are dying. We take Phoebe and leave.

As Michael and Phoebe and I walk toward the rental car I have an urge to double back and crouch under an open window, to hear Grace critique me. I am almost eager for it. If I get caught, I reason with myself, I can always say I dropped an earring or I'm admiring her garden. The part under the window.

I can always tell her the truth, which is that I have never matured.

Phoebe is a bright adolescent who says "It's OK" about everything.

Do you like your steak?

"It's OK."

How did you feel about the movie?

"It's OK."

What do you think of female genital mutilation?

"It's OK."

I don't feel what I think I'm supposed to be feeling about Phoebe. I feel indifferent. She's not making me love her.

I call Lana and she is definite.

"No," she says. "You won't feel anything. Neither will she. Maybe in a long time, something. Maybe."

I do like the way she giggles. It's more of a snort, really.

For the first time it occurs to me, no matter how honorary the title, I am going to be a stepmother. Sending the innocent children out to the dark forest, on the pretext of gathering wood. Instructing the hunter to remove the small, still beating heart, so that I might reign supreme in Michael's affections. The usual.

. . .

Ray called from Dallas today.

"Dusty died," he says. His voice sounds strange, as though some industrial accident has occurred, and now he, Ray, is flat.

He explains the circumstances of Dusty's death as if reading from a card. Every sentence or two he stops, and all I hear is his breath as he crushes back tears, which are coming inexplicably from somewhere inside the flatness.

This is what happened.

Dusty was in bed, with his sister Rhonda and her husband and Jim Bentley gathered around in chairs nearby. Bentley, who was Ray's college roommate, was telling a joke, when Dusty started to cough. The hospice nurse cleared the room. And then he died, choking on his own blood.

"Remind me not to invite Bentley to any more parties," Ray says before he hangs up.

I haven't cried. Because he's not gone. If he were gone, I would know it.

In Vermont, Phoebe and Michael and I go roller-skating at a rink. There is a group of incredibly beautiful young black girls from a local Salvation Army summer camp, skating happily. They go around and around, like stars.

I can't stop thinking about Dusty. Trying to absorb the fact of his death, which seems even more unbelievable because I wasn't there, because these small girls are screaming with glee and so obviously complete in themselves.

What I feel is a need to know he's all right. I've asked for a sign.

Michael and I went horseback riding with Phoebe on the world's oldest living horses this afternoon, and then spent the rest of the day at the small, quiet hotel pool.

Our air conditioner, which the hotel management says is brand-new, keeps shutting itself off. The men have come to fix it twice, shaking their heads and adjusting their caps on their heads. They don't understand what's wrong.

Perhaps this is the sign. Or it could be incompetence. I will know later, will request another sign. The first one wasn't strong enough.

Lunch with Michael's ex-wife. She served grilled ono and white Bordeaux on the veranda of her spacious home.

There is something intrinsically terrible about ex-wives. Their faces hoard knowledge. Yet at bone level I know she's had the worst of it. Michael has said he wasn't ready to be married at thirty-one, and I believe him. Second wives have the edges filed for them. Through the first marriage and the conflagration of the divorce, the men are pre-hobbled.

We played a little game, Grace and I. Each time I said something, she made no response. This, I saw early on, would be the sport. To see who could reveal the least to the other. Yet we had revealed everything by choosing the same man. I, of course, would lose. She knew that, which is why she had chosen the game. Michael would never have married a stupid woman.

It grew so quiet, and I was so obviously losing, having said several dozen words to her six or seven, that I found myself talking about Dusty. I mentioned that my friend the artist had died and how I was able to buy, yesterday, over the phone, at the very last minute, one of his sculptures before the executors came to cart everything away.

I said, "I wonder what it looks like."

Grace fiddled absently with her watchband, tightening it one notch.

"I bought it sight unseen," I said.

And she said nothing; she just looked up from her fine timepiece and blinked at me, as though trying to remember who I was.

Then her dogwood centerpiece toppled over and spilled all the wine. There was no wind, it just fell. I laughed. She ran for towels.

Dusty?

It is our last day here.

I was drying my hair this morning, using the hotel's hair dryer, as I have every day. With a loud crack! the electrical outlet short-circuited. When I unplugged the cord, the prongs were black.

He's out there. Free.

Weeping, I sat on the bed, with its awful pink-and-orange hotel bedspread.

I will never see him again. I repeat this fact, to cross the river.

They spread his ashes yesterday, back in Matador, Texas.

I could have flown standby, but I chose to stay here with Michael and Phoebe. It's Michael's birthday. We have Thai food, at his daughter's favorite restaurant. Pad Thai noodles with a candle, stealthily arranged by Phoebe.

When Michael blows out the candle, I think of Dusty. I experience a wave of guilt. Clearly I have failed him, not being there for the ceremony.

Then I hear him. Smoking a cigarette, exhaling with a long chuckling sigh.

"*Fuck* it, darlin'."

Always generous, he left his voice in my head.

When I get home, my mom wants to know all about Grace. I tell her how the first thing she mentioned to me, at our lunch, is how she met Camille Paglia and they had cocktails together. She had gone to see her read from her new book and had tickets to a private reception afterward at Gotham, where she had the fortune to be seated across from her. It's like she opened my head and chose the one thing I would really, really like to do, and then revealed she had already done it. Amazing. A gift, really. I can see why Michael loved her.

Then this morning I wake up crying about Dusty. I ask Michael to bring in his sculpture, so I can hold it as I lie in bed. He does.

I ask Michael, "Why Dusty? Why couldn't it be someone I don't like, or wouldn't miss."

I have several people in mind.

Michael says that he thinks there's a plan, a reason why this happened, that we don't get to know. He doesn't think it's any worse than being born, dying.

He says that Dusty is just going back to the place he was

before he was born. He says this and watches my face for improvement. At times like this it becomes absolutely clear to me that I can do without anything but Michael. He is the linchpin. This is the best and worst news I have ever received: I am once more eligible for loss.

Then he says, "They shouldn't call it death, it's bad PR. They should call it Stage B."

I hold him, so he doesn't get away.

I decided I am definitely keeping my name. I'm not even hyphenating. I feel extremely territorial, almost suspicious. As though there were someone trying to rub me out.

"Only you can rub you out," Reuben says. "You are the villain and the heroine, and you're everyone in the audience."

"Who is Michael?" I ask.

"He's your costar," Reuben says. Then he reconsiders.

"Who Michael is, is none of your business."

I called Ray today, to see how he was doing.

He said that what he mostly felt was how thankful he was to have known Dusty, that he got to spend twenty-eight years with him.

"I never had to be anything with Dusty," he said.

His voice sounds deep and low, like a tree bending against the wind. I realize this is how people age, by surviving.

Then he gets very serious.

"I want to ask you something. . . ."

I know what he is going to say.

"Um . . . do you think Dusty was in love with me?"

There is a small silence. I have known Ray since we were seven; this is the first time I've heard him stammer.

Ray says, "I mean I never thought of that, in all the time I knew him. He was just my best friend. He never did anything that would have made me think that."

That's love, is what I was thinking, the truest form.

Then Ray says, "I wish we had eighty-eight years."

When Dusty was alive, weeks would go by when I'd barely think of him. We only spoke every couple months. But now I see that he was an essential part of me. And there is nothing I can do about it. I just have to live without that part and accept the void where it was. Or make up something on my own, composed of him, to stuff in the hole.

I have his sculpture, on the kitchen table. A red figure embracing a blue figure, wood pitted and distressed, faces like Easter Island faces. His wedding gift.

September

*It seemed to me that the desire to get married—
which, I regret to say, I believe is basic and primal
in women—is followed almost immediately by an
equally basic and primal urge, which is to be single
again.*

NORA EPHRON

One month and seventeen days until the wedding.

I had a long Come to Jesus speech with Michael about helping. I described in detail my impending nervous breakdown unless he dove in almost immediately. I gave him a list of eight tasks, the same ones we decided on six months ago, written on the list that's hanging on the refrigerator. The list he completely ignored.

Then I went to the gym.

While on the treadmill I listened to the Fugees, where the MC sings, "If you let them kick you five times, they'll kick you five times / If you let them kick you three times, they'll kick you three times / If you let them kick you two times, they'll kick you two times / If you let them kick you once, they kick you once / But if you break off they motherfuckin' feet, ain't gonna be no more kickin' goin' on."

Everything costs a thousand dollars, except the things that cost more than a thousand dollars. That's information for anyone planning a wedding.

I booked the jazz quartet for our reception. I have not heard of them, but the saxophone player used to play with Ray Charles.

Ray Charles was referenced. Twelve hundred and seventy-five dollars.

Meanwhile Jill (Calgon . . . Take Me Away) called me at work, on her way to Fullerton on business. She is doing a project for Rosarita.

"I'm going into my ninety-first focus group on beans," she said.

She reminded me to send her the guest list for my wedding shower, which she is throwing for me in Mill Valley, where she lives with her dog Mishegoss. We're going to have a high tea with real silver and petits fours and watercress sandwiches and canapés.

"Don't try to stop me," she says.

Michael and I went to city hall for our marriage license today. We simply filled out a small form, wrote a check for sixty-nine dollars, and signed our names.

"We could walk next door and get married right now," Michael said. "Save a lot of money."

It seems almost magical. Prescription eyeglasses in about

an hour. I feel envious of the couples who are doing this. I imagine that they will enjoy a clean and unfettered transformation, and go on to live exceptionally smart lives.

Grace calls to talk to Michael about Phoebe, and I answer the phone.

She says, "You know I never did congratulate you." She sounds different.

Then, brightly, "Where are you going on your honeymoon?"

Who is this really? I want to ask. But I say Paris and Thanks! and Bye for now! and I hand the phone to Michael.

As I hear them speaking, I reflect on the fact that I don't want Grace to become a person.

She is in danger of becoming real now, of becoming someone I could know. Part of me feels pleased.

The other part says, *Shit.*

This morning we picked songs for the jazz quartet to play. I kept crying at the lyrics. Not just crying, wailing.

"Witchcraft" is going to be our first dance.

Everything I locked away and thought I couldn't have, it turns out I am going to have. I feel shocked.

I told that to Fiona, the Leigh-Woman, as she was altering my wedding dress last Saturday, and she got this very angry look, and said, "You *deserve* it." She looked as if she was going to throw something, but then she bent down and pinned the hem on my slip.

.   .   .

Lana came and spent the weekend with us, along with Isabel, who is eighteen months and keeps running around the house saying "Oh no. Oh no."

Isabel is the only baby I can abide, because I knew her before she was born. One day Lana called me up and said "Guess what?" and I said "You're pregnant." And started to cry.

Isabel kisses her own hand; she adores herself. She has a good name, and she's bald, which is fetching in a girl. She does magic tricks with her hands, striking dramatic poses, arms outstretched stiffly in front of her, eyes dancing.

Sometimes when she walks, she looks like a tiny and extremely busy mayor.

Lana and I watched the original *Titanic,* with Barbara Stanwyck, last night. Her husband, Clifton Webb, is this total bastard, but then when the ship goes down he turns into a hero again and she kisses him hard on the lips like she can't bear to lose him. Which she can't. But I notice she gets in the lifeboat anyway.

There's a scene in the beginning where the husband is shaving and Barbara Stanwyck is crying and wringing her hands and begging him not to callously disown their only son, and he says, "You're standing in my light."

That's marriage, is what I thought. That's how bad it can get.

I feel it is only natural to be afraid.

We all went to Rockaway Beach and Isabel went ballistic over a box of cookies. We'd give her one and put the box back in the knapsack, and before she even had that one chewed, she'd be screaming for the box again. When Lana left me alone with her, I immediately gave up and handed the whole box to her.

She knows already that it's not enough just to have a cookie. You have to control the cookies.

Lana and Isabel left this morning, to go back to New Mexico. Before they did, Lana said, "Michael's darling, by the way. He's great."

"I know," I said.

With her old trick of reading my mind, she matter-of-factly says, "You won't find better."

I feel enormously relieved to hear her say that.

Today while I was driving, a man cut me off and I screamed *"SCREW YOU ASSHOLE"* and then high-revved my engine with the clutch in. I wanted to drive my car over the top of his car.

It's two days before my period, but it's not just the PMS. And it's not just the wedding. Right behind that, hiding behind the chiffon veil, is the marriage, unknown and unknowable. The mine shaft of marriage. You may hit gold or you may be crushed when the ceiling collapses. And directly behind the marriage waits childbirth and spread hips and flat breasts and then right behind childbirth waits death. Waving, in a black tuxedo.

It's not just the PMS, although I imagine murderesses saying that too, screaming with chocolate-ringed mouths, waving bloody kitchen knives as they are hauled off to the electric chair. But between the PMS and the wedding and the marriage and the spreading and the flattening and the death, I am losing it. Whatever it is I had, or was supposed to hold on to.

I feel like someone, a very mean enemy, has poured kerosene over my head and lit it with a cherry bomb.

I think a good system would be to take one Valium every day for four days before my period, until after the wedding.

I have enough.

I saw Reuben and told him that Ilene was pummeling me with questions about the wedding and her hotel and did I see the room and when are we picking her up at the airport and how a shuttle is too expensive and how it is too bad that everyone from the wedding party isn't staying in the same hotel, and can she walk to David and Ruth's hotel and how many blocks is it and are there hills and do they give you breakfast at the hotel and what kind and did we book a room for Michael's cousin Lydia and her twin infants and how are we going to keep those babies out of direct sun during the wedding service? It takes seven minutes for a baby's brain to sustain permanent damage, she informs me.

I fear Ilene's voice on the answering machine, commanding us to call her. She doesn't just want Michael, anymore. She wants me. On some level I feel that she can kill me, if I step out of line. She can kill my happiness. She can do it with questions and eyebrows and sentences that trail off.

I told Reuben that despite the fact that she is seventy-five years old and ninety-five pounds and two thousand miles away in New York, right now the thought of a confrontation with Ilene is completely terrifying.

I also told him that she seems to be warming up for something big, some display of strength and magnificence that will place her at the center of the prewedding hysteria. I sense Ilene is gaining in power and will. I don't know what her next question or request will be; I only know that I will fall short and she will say, "That's all right, dear. It's not like this is Michael's first wedding. Now *that* was a wedding."

Meltdown.

In the end I was curled in a fetal position on the couch at 1 a.m., wishing I could find a way to somehow not feel. To not go through this.

I told Michael, "I can't do this. I can't get married. I can't do it right."

Crying silently and twisting my tee shirt into a ball, speaking in a voice almost like my own, not even raised or agitated. Just carefully explaining, in the alien voice.

"I'm not good enough. I just can't."

As if I were describing to him my inability to do a cartwheel. And the whole time I'm saying it I'm mildly surprised, because I always thought that if I wanted to, I could do one.

He went and got me a Valium, one of the blue ones, the ten milligram. The big guns. Then he made me drink a glass of water and he sat on the edge of the couch next to me and held my hand. I felt bathed by sheer relief at his presence. That and the Valium. Twelve left, plus the powder at the bottom of the bottle.

· · ·

I had a massage today, right before my wedding shower. I was lying on the table trying to relax and feel pampered and bridal, while simultaneously obsessing about the huppah poles which the local temple won't lend us because we're getting married on a Saturday, and how no one from my side of the family got the direction sheet in their invitations. My naked body was slick with Tranquility Time antistress aromatherapy oil and I'm consumed with whether everyone has directions, and whether once they receive them will they forget to bring them.

Pegge was kneading my back vertebra by vertebra, and I just wanted her to finish so I could call Michael and scrape it all onto his plate. I just want to whip out my cell phone and call him and make him deal with everything, but it's inside my locker. I thought I could hear it ringing. And the Indian flute music was being piped into the massage room, and my scalp was throbbing with anxiety and the bottoms of my feet were twitching uncontrollably. The Hopi flutes were playing and I wanted to jump off the table and scream like someone had ripped my talisman off, which they had. My talisman of being single and independent and not having to worry about whether we can get huppah poles from Ace Hardware, not having to obsess over whether my entire wedding party is going to end up at Sam's Anchor Grill eating lobster, having given up looking for the wedding.

Yesterday I told Reuben how I just wanted everyone in my family to drop off the face of the earth.

"That is how they would serve you best," he said, completely serious.

Then when I get home from the spa, I spend twenty minutes railing at Michael about all this when Lana and Yvonne call to announce they are going to be two hours late and that

I am also going to be two hours late because tradition demands that we all three arrive together to our twenty-year high-school reunion. Which happens to be tonight. The same day as my wedding shower.

I sit down on my bed moaning and half dressed and say to Michael, "I'm not going anywhere. I don't want to go anywhere."

It occurred to me if I just sat there long enough, I wouldn't have to deal with any of this. The enemy was movement.

The hot tub was full of white balloons.

For my bridal shower, Jill had hired two caterers and put out silver trays and sugar bowls and teapots, and at my seat there was a place card that said "The Bride Herself." There was a large blue china vessel full of ice and bottles of mineral water and champagne and white wine. And right then when I sat down at one of the tables she had set up in her garden, a West Indian caterer with a degree from Yale handed me a tray and said, "Crumpet?"

I don't deserve this, I thought, but Jill thinks I do, so I'll play along.

Right away, two of my divorced friends got into a conversation about how they knew they were doing the wrong thing when they walked down the aisle.

"I knew," they both said.

How? I wanted to ask. How did you know. I want desperately to cross-reference symptoms, but under the circumstances it doesn't seem appropriate. So instead we all sat in the garden and were barraged by tiny Gruyère quiches and homemade truffles and radish cream-cheese tarts and heart-shaped chocolate petit-fours. I kept wondering how I was going to repay Jill for all of this, but she seemed unconcerned. She reclined on a redwood chaise, wearing a huge yellow hat and telling stories about her three marriages, while the West Indian named Kenneth refilled our glasses, and I thought about how I could really enjoy this if I weren't getting married in five weeks. I could surely enjoy this magnificent sunset if my car weren't careening off a cliff.

Naturally I smiled and passed the butterballs. What I feel primarily about the final throes of engagement is it doesn't do to let people know how terrified you are. They can't handle it, is what I suspect.

Later I attended my twenty-year high-school reunion and spent the evening avoiding the same people I avoided in high school (Alan Wappo and Fred Rooney) and coveting the attention of the same ones I coveted (Martin Neuberger and Brian Struthers).

One classmate who was newly divorced and who always wears Ralph Lauren Polo shirts sat next to me at dinner. He told me how lovely I looked and how happy he was for me that I was finally getting married. "Finally," was the word he used. Then without missing a beat, he leaned forward with this very doubting, soulful look and asked, "What do you think about monogamy?"

And all I could think about was how Dusty had recently told me that this man's wife had found a box of condoms in his suitcase when he came home from a trip supposedly to see his brother in Chicago. A *box*. Which was shortly before she filed for divorce and relieved him of everything he owned. "Either he was cheatin'," said Dusty, "or he is *way* too close to his brother."

And although I couldn't tell the Ralph Lauren Polo man what I thought about monogamy, which is that I believe in it, even though, as with God, I'm not 100 percent sure it exists, I definitely wanted to say something about the box of condoms in his suitcase, because it seemed that was only fair. I definitely wanted to thank him for bringing up the subject of imminent betrayal during the heartbeat before my wedding.

But instead I just shook my head slowly while he smiled his beatific, turtlelike smile and waited for my answer, a light and airy expression on his face. The face of someone urinating in the country club pool.

I go to pick up my wedding dress from Fiona the Leigh-Woman.

It fits well. I still wish I had lost more weight. But then part of me just says, Well, you'll be dead soon anyway. The other part of me says, You look lovely. I mood swing between Cinderella and Rumplestiltskin.

I put back on my regular clothes, which seem like a costume now. Back in her living room, Fiona sits me down and says, "These are my rules: Aspirin. A second set of hose. You don't know what's going to happen to the second set of hose, so . . . clear nail polish. And a needle and thread."

She hands me a small white pillbox with a needle and thread in it and a picture of Jesus on the front. She holds a tiny blue flower, sewn of cloth, in her other hand.

"Is Jesus OK?" she asks. "Some people are offended by Jesus. If so, I can cover him with this blue flower."

"Jesus is fine," I say.

She puts the flower back in her pocket; I finger the small white round box. Jesus smiles up at me. He never got married, is what I am thinking. All the really great ones don't.

"OK, so tuck that in your purse."

I do this. I feel much more prepared.

"Now. You're going to get your shoes today. I want you to wear them at home, as much as you possibly can between now and the wedding. And then I want you to go out into the street and scuff them.

"Because let me tell you, you are going to fall down."

When she says "fall down," I hear "fail."

I write down the rules. I write down everything she says.

"Well, that's it," she declares. "Good luck."

She is seated with her hands folded in her lap, staring straight ahead at me, as though I am about to dematerialize to a secret mission on Pluto.

When we stand up, I give her a big hug. My cheek is against her long hair, which smells like pine. I pull away and walk across the front lawn, carrying my wedding dress in a white plastic zipper bag.

I don't want to leave her little ramshackle house. It seems to me to be the center of some great concentration of wisdom.

But I do leave. As I am leaving everything.

Last night I took three Sominex just to attempt sleep. My body ached as if every muscle were clenched in anticipation of a head-on collision. What if you get married and you hate it. What if you have an affair. Would he leave you, or would you stay together? What if he has an affair. What if he doesn't; does that mean he's finally old? What if he turns into your father. Sitting in an armchair looking bitter and hating everyone on television. Consider how Beth and Robert broke up. He was an older man too. Exactly eight years older, just like Michael and me. What if Michael is Robert and ends up living on a houseboat in Santa Barbara, just like Robert? Would I be relieved like Beth is?

I don't want to be relieved. I want to care. But I'm too numb and we haven't had sex in three weeks and my shoulders are throbbing like a giant bit them.

What if he goes bald. What if we can't find a house. What if I can't have a baby.

What if I can. Your life is *over*, sugar.

What if you buy a house and get pregnant and lose your job and have a baby, and you end up hating him. Fornicating with handymen while he's at work to get back at him for ruining your life and taking away the expense accounts and impromptu trips to New York and London and Mondrian Hotel room service. What then.

I worry and wonder, deep in the tomb-silent night.

I want to go backward to when I was still longing for marriage and felt it would fix everything. Things were simple and unfulfilled then, like the night before you begin a vacation, a perfect canvas of time unblemished by events. It's like when Isaac Mizrahi said whenever he goes to Paris he just wants to have a cup of coffee and go back home.

This morning I told Michael I was tired and I didn't want to go to work, go on our honeymoon, or even go to the kitchen. I didn't want to worry about whether he's sent his mother a birthday gift or whether the caterer will remember to return the bud vases to the florist or whether we took the recycling out for pickup because it's Thursday. What I want to do is be alone, and cease taking care of anything. Anything.

But I am going to get married, because it is time and because I don't want anyone else to have him.

Four weeks until I walk the aisle. Something dreadful happened when it went below thirty days. Less than a month is real. I want to do it, though. I do.

I do. Jesus it really comes down to that, doesn't it.

I wonder now why having a rabbi seemed a good idea. He's just going to make it more serious, with that white beard.

I want a woman minister. A lesbian woman named Heron. Someone a vengeful God won't take too seriously. Someone I could laugh off later and say, Oh we were just kidding. You didn't think we were serious did you?

It's not just the rabbi: I have a series of regrets. Too many to go into. People I invited, people I didn't invite, and the fact that I didn't, say, marry Jackson Kent. Or one of the Baldwin brothers. Or Wesley Snipes.

It just hit me that I am never going to have a black man. The black man window is closed.

I am never going to have another twenty-five-year-old. I don't necessarily want them, but I want the option of them. I want their window left open.

What I've heard, actually, is that marriage kills sex. That after you get married, you never actually have sex again. First frequency goes and then oral sex goes and then it all goes. I've heard.

In that case I can't be expected to be ready. I'm a young woman. Thirty-six is still young. Except for a first marriage. Thirty-six is far too old for a first marriage.

Maybe I can get off on a technicality.

This morning Michael is talking on the phone when he covers the receiver and says to me, "Your Blue Cross is not applicable in Europe and is not honored."

We are spending eight days in France for our honeymoon. He has just signed himself up for supplemental European health insurance coverage and is wanting to sign me up too. I know this is a ridiculous waste of money. I smile and nod.

"There's someone else I want to put on the medical insurance policy," he says into the phone. "My future wife," he says, and actually giggles.

When he hangs up, I ask him if he thinks we should also bring two miner's helmets, just in case the sun explodes.

"You won't laugh when you're lying down there with a broken leg paying ten thousand dollars," he says.

"Lying down where?" I ask.

"Some hospital in France." He says it as though there will be buckets full of shoes with feet still in them, and no anesthesia. Just men with berets and rusty saws.

"Go ahead, laugh," he says.

I do. It feels good.

Nineteen days until the wedding.

I'm not ready. I know, because I want to laugh hysterically when people ask me if I'm ready.

I'm not ready to be old, or bored, or fat. All of which I believe marriage represents.

I'm not ready to be my mother. I just started looking good. Not my mother, not yet. Not ever.

If I get married I'll have to have a baby right away. They'll make me. I am not sure who they are, only that they exist.

I'll have to have a baby, which will make me a mother. Beyond repair. Pot holders and kitchen magnets and big bras. Good God.

I'm not ready never to have my own apartment again. I'm not ready to erase all possibility of a pink-and-red bathroom, which I am never going to have if I get married.

I'm not ready to watch Michael grow old, and die. I want to remember him as he is right now, with shiny black hair and muscles and his own teeth. I'm not ready for dentures in a glass by the bed and stocking caps and brown slippers and gray alien skin.

I don't want to go forward, I just decided. I would like to go sideways. Revisit recent highlights.

The day at Stinson Beach when Michael wore that blue-and-white bandanna on his head. The trip to Boston for his brother David's wedding. The long tight black velvet dress I wore and Michael in a tuxedo and that room at the Hilton with the tall maroon curtains. I had a good haircut, too. One of the only good haircuts I've ever had.

I would like to go back there. To good haircuts and being thirty-five and tight black size-8 dresses and hotel rooms and room service hors d'oeuvres and other people's weddings.

If I am honest with myself, I wasn't happy then either, I remember. I was secretly miserable.

Because I wanted to get married.

October

In the end maybe what marriage offered was the
determination of one's burial site.

JANE HAMILTON

We go to dinner with Lesli and her husband, Henry, at
Gordon Biersch for my thirty-seventh birthday. I examine
Michael from across the table. He seems strange, but nice.
The boyfriend of someone I know but not too well. I could
steal him away from her, if I decided to.

I talk to Lesli, and Michael talks to Henry.

I sanctimoniously order the grilled *ahi* which arrives raw,
like slices of human flesh. It's so disgusting I can only mar-
vel at it. I feel beyond food, although alcohol is definitely my
friend.

We drink two bottles of ZD Chardonnay. It may be that I
am trying to pickle myself, preserving the old me. Find a big
jug and just float.

When we arrive home I grab the phone and go out back
to chain-smoke.

I call Jill and tell her I feel I'm slipping away. The death of the maiden, as Reuben would say, which makes it sound like a ridiculously youthful experience. I haven't been a maiden for twenty years. This maiden crap just pisses me off.

What's perishing is me. The me who was single. The me who was me, for as long as I have known me.

"I'm dying," I say to Jill.

I wait for her to tell me I'm being ridiculous.

"I know," she says.

"I am ET lying in the ditch," I murmur. "And nobody is going to save me, no kids on flying bicycles. I'm just going to die there."

We laugh.

I am so very afraid.

I maintain a conviction that I am the only one who has experienced this. The rest of the engaged world, I fear, is doing fine. Just fine.

As I write this I can hear the crazy South African land-lady outside telling her feather-duster dog, *"Sit down. Get up. Sit down. Get up."*

I see Reuben and tell him that it is now twelve days until the wedding and it isn't at all the way I thought it would be. At all.

I feel angry, as though he is on the Board.

I tell Reuben how ugly it is to have changed places with Michael. How just when he stops being afraid of marriage, I start. I tell him how I realize now that it is no accident that I haven't gotten married before. I used to think it was an accident, an error. That I hadn't met the right person. But now I know I didn't get married because I didn't want to. And I know why. Because it feels horrible.

Reuben says, "It's like Disneyland, where you go into a dark tunnel and the monsters jump out at you and the man with the head of an alligator, but it's not real."

"Why isn't it real?" I ask.

"Because they're all projections."

"Oh yeah," I say. I knew that.

"It's the Tunnel of Horrors," Reuben says. Grinning.

The Tunnel of Horrors. A very real place. I feel I could reach out and touch its clammy sides and hear the laughter of the crazy gondolier.

"I think you can escape it," Reuben says. "I think it's like an evil spirit." He claws at the air with one hand as he says this.

I wonder what Reuben does for fun, I think. He seems to be having fun now. I wonder if I am having fun. I suspect that in some sick way I am, just like on a roller coaster. Putting my arms up in the air and screaming.

"Projections," I say.

"That's right," he says.

I feel like I'm learning Spanish by phonograph. I keep repeating the word for "artichoke," but I know I really can't speak Spanish.

Then I hand him the directions to the wedding. He's coming.

I was looking at Michael's feet last night and they look just like Picasso's feet. A small, troubling thing.

Ten days until the wedding. I'm off work now, until after the honeymoon.

I call Lana. I tell her that I hope what I'm feeling is normal.

"It's a sentence," she admits, talking about marriage. "More so for a woman than for a man."

"But it's good," she says, with equal conviction.

"The moments that are great are spread out more. Plus you get these reality checks; like you're ill and he makes you soup, and brings it to you in bed. Or you hear about someone whose husband is sixty and still screws around with secretaries, and you feel so blessed."

"Administrative assistants," I say. She ignores me.

"You have to take the whole package. You can't get Liam Neeson *and* George Clooney."

"I know," I say.

"You take the package. Like, Michael has that great East Coast Jewish thing going on. See, Raul doesn't have that. I miss that. He has other things I like about him. But sometimes that quality that you like about them is the same one that shreds at you like a paper cut."

"Yes," is all I can muster up. I feel a mass of paper cuts. One big slice down the center, by the world's biggest envelope.

Lana says, "There are times when I just look at Raul and say *Stop*. He hasn't done anything, but I am just so aware of what he's about to do."

"Exactly," I say.

"But you don't want to ruin this time. You've waited for this a long time, and you and Michael are great together."

"We are?" I ask. I thought she was going somewhere else with this.

"You are."

I ask her the final incendiary question. I ask her if Michael's good-looking. I need her to be my eyes, now that I've gone insane.

"He's darling. And he's sexy," she says.

He is. I know this intellectually.

"I wouldn't lie," she adds. "You're in such a good time, Eve. Just move forward."

Ah yes. Movement. But boxcars move too. Bombs fall; women release the emergency brake on minivans full of toddlers.

Then she pivots. She says, "Besides, there are no guarantees in life. . . ." Her voice trails off deliciously. "What the years will bring. You don't really know how long you'll have together."

I picture myself at Michael's funeral, in a sheer black chiffon blouse. High necked, with palazzo pants. Some neutral lipstick.

"We could all end up single," she says. "Look at my mother. Look at Aunt Daisie."

Lana's aunt Daisie always swore she would outlive her husband, Frank, and eventually retire with her sister Eleanor, but she died at sixty-six, leaving Lana's mother, Eleanor, alone. Who did outlive her husband, along with outliving Aunt Daisie. Silver-haired high-cheekboned Eleanor the Impeccable, who recently told me she would like to meet a man who was like Michael. This also weighs in on his side.

"In any case," Lana says, "I'd rather be questioning my marriage than just questioning my connections with people.

Wondering whether some man is going to call me because I slept with him. Or didn't."

"But you have Isabel already," I say. "You have dividends."

I think she is going to say, No, that's not the way to look at it, but she says, "Then maybe you should just have a baby right away. Get pregnant and get it over with, and not wait a year."

I flash on Lana sideswiping a bus as she drove her very first car, a white Mustang. We looked at each other, said "Get the hell out of here!" and tore ass. We never got caught.

I love Lana. There is safety with Lana.

She continues, "I have always been an advocate of making many changes at the same time and getting them all over with in one lump. A baby," she says. "That's another huge step. Everything's a huge step," she says.

Then she says, "For me, I did it by not looking at it."

I realize she is not talking about having Isabel, but marrying Raul. Maybe she is talking about having Isabel, too. She really is touched. But there's no one else I would rather be talking to, not even Camille Paglia. Who also never married.

"I think one reason why you're doubting is it's safe now," she says.

"Why?" I ask.

"Because it's so close." She explains: "You can't really call it off, it's too late. So it's very safe to have doubts now. . . .

"In other words, we can all put on black turtlenecks and smoke cigarettes and drink espresso and lead a heavy discussion about getting married like *'Fuck*, it's not the way I expected it to be . . .' and then it's like 'Oh by the way I'm getting married tomorrow. . . .'"

She's right.

"Do you have anything else?" I ask.

"Well . . ."

She thinks about it.

"It's sort of a cheap way out, but look at all the unhappy people."

"I know," I say. Thinking about all the unhappy people is actually extremely helpful.

"Tell me again how great Michael is," I instruct.

"He's great," she says.

"I know," I say miserably.

Lana says, in the voice I imagine she uses on her tenth-grade students, "I know you know, but you need me to feed it back to you."

I woke up this morning to the sound of rain.

We have no contingency for rain at our wedding site.

I cry and can't stop. Also, I can't get out of bed. Because of the rain. The rain that is raining out of season, exactly eight days before my wedding. My *outdoor* wedding. Which I now see was complete lunacy.

Michael says, "Don't worry about things you can't control."

I gaze at him as he calmly prepares himself for work. I would like to throw something at his head. I would like to knock his glasses off.

I begin to softly keen. He sits down on the edge of the bed.

"What else are you worried about?" he asks.

"Divorce," I say. There. I said it. "My father was married twice; my mother twice. That's four marriages and two people," I say. It seems a very strong argument.

"Let's get married first and then we can get divorced, OK sweetie?" he says.

I put on my wedding shoes last night, with thick socks like Fiona said. They suddenly feel two sizes too small. They were fine in the store. They tricked me.

I hobble around the house. Michael sees the shoes, but I don't care. We won't have any good luck anyway.

I think about backing out. But shoes don't seem enough of a reason.

My uncle Wallace is in town, all the way from Missouri. My father's brother, whom I haven't seen since I was seven. He'll be at the wedding. What I imagine is that my father will use his eyes.

Today I had a manicure and a facial. As the women were rubbing oils into my arms, I closed my eyes and thought, It's beginning. The ritual. Afterward I bought a cream-colored pair of size-9 shoes to bring to the wedding, in case my feet start to hurt. I have, I see, some modicum of control. I can control shoes.

Later at the gym, I pick up a *Chronicle*. The weather forecast says fair and sunny on Saturday. I whoop out loud when I read it.

When my father used to take me to the racetrack, he taught me how to watch the odds board, how not to bet until the very last minute. We'd stand and watch the odds change, together.

I will walk alone down the aisle. Deeply flawed, he can't be replaced.

Michael has a dream that he is looking at a house for us, when he finds out that I own an elephant. He has to figure out how to get the elephant moved, where the elephant is going to sleep, et cetera. After he wakes up, he carefully explains to me how, once inside the prospective house, he climbed a ladder and poked his hand up through the ceiling to see how high the roof went, so that it could accommodate everyone.

It strikes me that this is the best kind of man to marry. The kind who will take care not just of me, but my elephant.

Union Square, a few last-minute items.

I walked down Powell Street, grinning like a fool. I can't seem to stop.

The fear has been ebbing the last few days and now it's almost completely gone.

So, the ebullience comes back, two days before your wedding. The boomerang effect. Something else no one tells you about.

They should parachute this information into the major cities.

Grace let Phoebe come, at the last minute. Michael wept when he found out. Picked her up at the airport in a limo, the same limo we'll be renting for the wedding. There is a symmetry to this.

Tonight was the rehearsal dinner. It was in the Tony Bennett Room at Fior d'Italia. Lana and Raul and Isabel and Beth and Lesli and Henry and Jill and Yvonne and Phoebe and Michael's brother, David, and his wife, Ruth, and her mother and cousin and my brother, Mark, and my mother, Bea, and Don all sat in a private room with dozens of framed pictures of Tony Bennett. A small grouchy Italian man in a tuxedo served us tricolored pasta and prawns and veal cutlets.

Michael sat at the head of the long table, and Phoebe sat to his right, and I sat to his left. Like Satan.

Lana was right next to me. She wore black cashmere with a faux-fur collar, and I wore a new hat and the gold velveteen dress that Michael loves. Bea and Don gave us two heavy silver serving pieces with our initials engraved on the handle, along with the date of our wedding. 10·19·96.

Tomorrow.

I woke up and looked out the window. Sunny.

I pick Lana up at the Capri Motel and we drive to the wedding site in my car, which I park near the grounds. A getaway vehicle, I can't help but think. Should the need arise.

In a small informal ceremony, we each knock back a Valium with orange juice. I give her the rest of the bottle, as a bridesmaid gift.

The wedding site was almost empty, unperturbed. A two-story Victorian perched on the edge of the bay. We walk around the terrace, through the back door. The flowers had already arrived, and the cake. I wanted to stay and stare at them, but then within minutes the caterers were arriving and then my mother came and Mark, and the piano was being delivered and people were shouting that it was after eleven o'clock and I had to go upstairs and start getting ready, immediately.

When I ran back downstairs for my purse, I saw a silver-haired man with familiar blue eyes. It was my uncle Wallace. He had come early. After we embraced I realized I had been waiting for him. Because the moment we parted I thought, *Now.*

And I went upstairs with Yvonne and Lana and Beth and applied my makeup, very methodically, trying to get everything just right and not botch the liner on my lips so I look like a mime. And the minutes started speeding up and I couldn't find my earrings or my hair spray, but Yvonne found the earrings and Beth lent me her hair spray and I barked orders at them and they didn't get mad, they just said yes, yes and scurried about getting me things. When I suddenly became thirsty, Lana read my mind at that exact moment and brought me water.

Then it was 11:55 and the photographer came in with an assistant and a huge round silver reflector board to take pictures of me in the small upstairs bathroom, which was bathed in sun. And then Lana stepped in and took my hands and said, "You look so beautiful."

I choked and said, "Don't make me cry." "I won't, I won't," she said, and she took me into her strong arms. The photographer is getting it all, hovering around like a bee, finally flitting off downstairs to torture someone else.

And then it is just Lana and me, because Yvonne and Beth have gone to hold the huppah poles.

I can hear muffled confusion downstairs. No one knows when they are supposed to go down the aisle; they are audibly crashing around like Keystone Cops. I am whispering obscenities, wondering aloud why we had a rehearsal dinner if no one was going to pay attention. I am pacing and wringing my hands and Lana is saying, "Take deep breaths" and asking, "Are you all right?"

And I lie and say that I am. My whole body is shaking and I seem to be standing next to myself, wondering why I am so afraid. It's not like I have to do anything. Luckily Lana is still upstairs with me, because she is second to the last in the procession. My matron of honor.

I look out the shuttered window at the top of the stairs and I see Yvonne and Beth and Jill struggling with the huppah, trying to untangle it. I would have laughed if it were someone else's wedding. But the rabbi directed them and finally it was up; the huppah was in place. Then the rabbi explained the meanings of the seven blessings and the huppah to the wedding guests. How it was a house that could go anywhere, a house with no walls, able to invite everyone in.

The music starts to play. My brother is playing Handel's *Largo*. As in a dream, I recognize the melody. The processional is beginning.

Lana has to go down. She is carrying her bouquet and wearing the same dress she married Raul in. I feel abandoned as I watch her rose-colored hat descend. Then it is just me, waiting at the top of the spindly spiral staircase. And for the first time, I realize that the bride is left alone to come last.

I am terrified that Michael will see me before he is supposed to. And then the marriage will fail. It all hinges on me, on waiting long enough.

I go down the stairs, pausing at each one. I clutch the banister. When I get to the bottom, I turn the corner, and I see that it's all right. I've done it right: Michael is just in front of the huppah, waiting for me.

And the expression on his face. Let me memorize it. Let me never forget it.

I grow aware of the others, the wedding guests. Standing in small rows in the sun, like wheat. They all turn around at once, to look at me. Their faces are pure hope. My immediate impulse is to burst into tears. I will myself not to.

Something more than the music is in my ears, a humming that is my father and Leigh and Dusty, and I think, This is what it must be like to die. I smile, pressing my lips together to stop the trembling.

I take a step. My veil lifts in the breeze. A sail.

I take another step.

When I reach Michael, he holds his arm out to me, as if we are about to dance.

And what I do is, I take it.

Acknowledgments

Nothing happens without several people in New York. My agent, Kim Witherspoon, showed intrepid care in making sure the material found a home. Immense gratitude to Jordan Pavlin and everyone at Knopf; thank you Sonny for laughing. I cannot imagine this or anything else without my excellent husband, Mark Friedman; appreciation is also owed to my newborn son, Pablo, a good sleeper. For various wildly disparate reasons I am indebted to Augusten Burroughs, Andrew Robinson, Jill Murray, Dee Alexich, Ken Woodard, my English professors at Berkeley, Gayle Finnamore, and the late Donnie Hunt; may there be Diet Dr Pepper in heaven, and may it be the old recipe.

Permissions Acknowledgments

A Note About the Author

Suzanne Finnamore lives in northern California with her husband and her son, Pablo. *Otherwise Engaged* is her first novel.

A Note on the Type

This book was set in Bodoni, a typeface named after Giambattista Bodoni (1740–1813), the celebrated printer and type designer of Parma. The Bodoni types of today were designed not as faithful reproductions of any one of the Bodoni fonts but rather as a composite, modern version of the Bodoni manner. Bodoni's innovations in type style included a greater degree of contrast in the thick and thin elements of the letters and a sharper and more angular finish of details.

Composed by Stratford Publishing Services,
Brattleboro, Vermont
Printed and bound by Haddon Craftsmen,
Bloomsburg, Pennsylvania
Designed by Virginia Tan